THE BEACH BOOK

BEACH

THE BEACH BOOK

Published in the UK by
Dorling Kindersley Limited
80 Strand, London WC2R ORL
www.dk.com
in association with

**MELCHER
MEDIA**

124 West 13th Street
New York, NY 10011
www.melcher.com

PUBLISHER: Charles Melcher
EDITOR IN CHIEF: Duncan Bock
PROJECT MANAGER: Megan Worman
PUBLISHING MANAGER: Bonnie Eldon
PRODUCTION DIRECTOR: Andrea Hirsh
EDITORIAL ASSISTANT: Lindsey Stanberry

DESIGNED BY *Ph.D*

Copyright © 2005 Melcher Media, Inc.

DuraBook™, patent no. 6,773,034, is
a trademark of Melcher Media, Inc. The
DuraBook™ format utilizes revolutionary
technology and is completely waterproof and
highly durable.

09 08 07 06   10 9 8 7 6 5 4 3 2
Printed in China

A CIP catalogue record for this book is available from the
British Library.

ISBN-13: 978-1-59591-003-5
ISBN-10:   1-59591-003-4

First Edition

CONTENTS

THE SHELL COLLECTOR *by* ANTHONY DOERR

*Originally from Cleveland, Ohio, ANTHONY DOERR
(b. 1973) has lived in Africa and New Zealand. His
acclaimed first collection of short stories,* The Shell
Collector, *earned Doerr the Rome Prize in 2004. Set
on the shores of Kenya, the unforgettable title story is
about a blind hermit whose esoteric knowledge of seashells leads to a crisis at once miraculous and deadly.*

T

HE SHELL COLLECTOR was scrubbing limpets at his
sink when he heard the water taxi come scraping over the reef.
He cringed to hear it—its hull grinding the calices of finger corals
and the tiny tubes of pipe organ corals, tearing the flower and fern
shapes of soft corals, and damaging shells too: punching holes in
olives and murexes and spiny whelks, in *Hydatina physis* and *Turris
babylonia*. It was not the first time people tried to seek him out.

He heard their feet splash ashore and the taxi motor off, back
to Lamu, and the light singsong pattern of their knock. Tumaini,
his German shepherd, let out a low whine from where she was
crouched under his sleeping cot. He dropped a limpet into the sink,
wiped his hands and went, reluctantly, to greet them.

They were both named Jim, overweight reporters from a New
York tabloid. Their handshakes were slick and hot. He poured them
chai. They occupied a surprising amount of space in the kitchen.

They said they were there to write about him: they would stay only two nights, pay him well. How did $10,000 American sound? He pulled a shell from his shirt pocket—a cerith—and rolled it in his fingers. They asked about his childhood: did he really shoot caribou as a boy? Didn't he need good eyes for that?

He gave them truthful answers. It all held the air of whim, of unreality. These two big Jims could not actually be at his table, asking him these questions, complaining of the stench of dead shellfish. Finally they asked him about cone shells and the strength of cone venom, about how many visitors had come. They asked nothing about his son.

All night it was hot. Lightning marbled the sky beyond the reef. From his cot he heard siafu feasting on the big men and heard them claw themselves in their sleeping bags. Before dawn he told them to shake out their shoes for scorpions and when they did one tumbled out. He heard its tiny scrapings as it skittered under the refrigerator.

He took his collecting bucket and clipped Tumaini into her harness, and she led them down the path to the reef. The air smelled like lightning. The Jims huffed to keep up. They told him they were impressed he moved so quickly.

"Why?"

"Well," they murmured, "you're blind. This path ain't easy. All these thorns."

Far off, he heard the high, amplified voice of the muezzin in Lamu calling prayer. "It's Ramadan," he told the Jims. "The people don't eat when the sun is above the horizon. They drink only chai until sundown. They will be eating now. Tonight we can go out if you like. They grill meat in the streets."

By noon they had waded a kilometer out, onto the great curved spine of the reef, the lagoon slopping quietly behind them, a low sea breaking in front. The tide was coming up. Unharnessed now, Tumaini stood panting, half out of the water on a mushroom-shaped dais of rock. The shell collector was stooped, his fingers middling, quivering, whisking for shells in a sandy trench. He snatched up a broken spindle shell, ran a fingernail over its incised spirals. "*Fusinus colus*," he said.

Automatically, as the next wave came, the shell collector raised his collecting bucket so it would not be swamped. As soon as the wave passed he plunged his arms back into sand, his fingers probing an alcove between anemones, pausing to identify a clump of brain coral, running after a snail as it burrowed away.

One of the Jims had a snorkeling mask and was using it to look underwater. "Lookit these blue fish," he gasped. "Lookit that *blue*."

The shell collector was thinking, just then, of the indifference of nematocysts. Even after death the tiny cells will discharge their poison—a single dried tentacle on the shore, severed eight days, stung a village boy last year and swelled his legs. A weeverfish bite bloated a man's entire right side, blacked his eyes, turned him dark purple. A stone fish sting corroded the skin off the sole of the shell collector's own heel, years ago, left the skin smooth and printless. How many urchin spikes, broken but still spurting venom, had he squeezed from Tumaini's paw? What would happen to these Jims if a banded sea snake came slipping up between their fat legs? If a lion fish was dropped down their collars?

"Here is what you came to see," he announced, and pulled the snail—a cone—from its collapsing tunnel. He spun it and balanced its flat end on two fingers. Even now its poisoned proboscis was nosing forward, searching him out. The Jims waded noisily over.

"This is a geography cone," he said. "It eats fish."

"*That* eats fish?" one of the Jims asked. "But my pinkie's bigger."

"This animal," said the shell collector, dropping it into his bucket, "has twelve kinds of venom in its teeth. It could paralyze you and drown you right here."

THIS ALL STARTED WHEN a malarial Seattle-born Buddhist named Nancy was stung by a cone shell in the shell collector's kitchen. It crawled in from the ocean, slogging a hundred meters under coconut palms, through acacia scrub, bit her and made for the door.

Or maybe it started before Nancy, maybe it grew outward from the shell collector himself, the way a shell grows, spiraling upward from the inside, whorling around its inhabitant, all the while being worn down by the weathers of the sea.

The Jims were right: the shell collector did hunt caribou. Nine years old in Whitehorse, Canada, and his father would send the boy leaning out the bubble canopy of his helicopter in cutting sleet to cull sick caribou with a scoped carbine. But then there was choroideremia and degeneration of the retina; in a year his eyesight was tunneled, spattered with rainbow-colored halos. By twelve, when his father took him four thousand miles south, to Florida, to see a specialist, his vision had dwindled into darkness.

The ophthalmologist knew the boy was blind as soon as he walked through the door, one hand clinging to his father's belt, the other arm held straight, palm out, to stiff-arm obstacles. Rather than examine him—what was left to examine?—the doctor ushered him into his office, pulled off the boy's shoes and walked him out the back door down a sandy lane onto a spit of beach. The boy had never seen sea and he struggled to absorb it: the blurs that were waves, the smears that were weeds strung over the tideline, the smudged yolk of sun. The doctor showed him a kelp bulb, let him break it in his hands and scrape its interior with his thumb. There were many such discoveries: a small horseshoe crab mounting a larger one in the wavebreak, a fistful of mussels clinging to the damp underside of rock. But it was wading ankle deep, when his toes came upon a small round shell no longer than a segment of his thumb, that the boy was truly changed. His fingers dug the shell up, he felt the sleek egg of its body, the toothy gap of its aperture. It was the most elegant thing he'd ever held. "That's a mouse cowry," the doctor said. "A lovely find. It has brown spots, and darker stripes at its base, like tiger-stripes. You can't see it, can you?"

But he could. He'd never seen anything so clearly in his life. His fingers caressed the shell, flipped and rotated it. He had never felt anything so smooth—had never imagined something could possess such deep polish. He asked, nearly whispering: "Who *made* this?" The shell was still in his hand, a week later, when his father pried it out, complaining of the stink.

Overnight his world became shells, conchology, the phylum *Mollusca*. In Whitehorse, during the sunless winter, he learned Braille, mail-ordered shell books, turned up logs after thaws to root for wood snails. At sixteen, burning for the reefs he had discovered in books like *The Wonders of Great Barrier*, he left Whitehorse for good and crewed sailboats through the tropics: Sanibel Island, St. Lucia, the Batan Islands, Colombo, Bora Bora, Cairns, Mombassa, Moorea. All this blind. His skin went brown, his hair white. His fingers, his senses, his mind—all of him—obsessed over the geometry of exoskeletons, the sculpture of calcium, the evolutionary rationale for ramps, spines, beads, whorls, folds. He learned to identify a shell by flipping it up in his hand; the shell spun, his fingers assessed its form, classified it: *Ancilla, Ficus, Terebra*. He returned to Florida, earned a bachelor's in biology, a Ph.D. in malacology. He circled the equator; got terribly lost in the streets of Fiji; got robbed in Guam and again in the Seychelles; discovered new species of bivalves, a new family of tusk shells, a new *Nassarius*, a new *Fragum*.

Four books, three Seeing Eye shepherds, and a son named Josh later, he retired early from his professorship and moved to a thatch-roofed kibanda just north of Lamu, Kenya, one hundred kilometers south of the equator in a small marine park in the remotest elbow of the Lamu Archipelago. He was fifty-eight years old. He had realized, finally, that he would only understand so much, that malacology only led him downward, to more questions. He had never comprehended the endless variations of design: Why this lattice ornament? Why these fluted scales, these lumpy nodes? Ignorance was, in the end, and in so many ways, a privilege: to find a shell, to feel it, to understand only on some unspeakable level why it bothered to be so lovely. What joy he found in that, what utter mystery.

Every six hours the tides plowed shelves of beauty onto the beaches of the world, and here he was, able to walk out into it, thrust his hands into it, spin a piece of it between his fingers. To gather up seashells—each one an amazement—to know their names, to drop them into a bucket: this was what filled his life, what overfilled it.

Some mornings, moving through the lagoon, Tumaini splashing comfortably ahead, he felt a nearly irresistible urge to bow down.

BUT THEN, TWO YEARS AGO, there was this twist in his life, this spiral which was at once inevitable and unpredictable, like the aperture in a horn shell. (Imagine running a thumb down one, tracing its helix, fingering its flat spiral ribs, encountering its sudden, twisting opening.) He was sixty-three, moving out across the shadeless beach behind his kibanda, poking a beached sea cucumber with his toe, when Tumaini yelped and skittered and dashed away, galloping downshore, her collar jangling. When the shell collector caught up, he caught up with Nancy, sunstroked, incoherent, wandering the beach in a khaki travel suit as if she had dropped from the clouds, fallen from a 747. He took her inside and laid her on his cot and poured warm chai down her throat. She shivered awfully; he radioed Dr. Kabiru, who boated in from Lamu.

"A fever has her," Dr. Kabiru pronounced, and poured seawater over her chest, swamping her blouse and the shell collector's floor. Eventually her fever fell, the doctor left, and she slept and did not wake for two days. To the shell collector's surprise no one came looking for her—no one called; no water taxis came speeding into the lagoon ferrying frantic American search parties.

As soon as she recovered enough to talk she talked tirelessly, a torrent of personal problems, a flood of divulged privacies. She'd been coherent for a half hour when she explained she'd left a husband and kids. She'd been naked in her pool, floating on her back,

12

when she realized that her life—two children, a three-story Tudor, an Audi wagon—was not what she wanted. She'd left that day. At some point, traveling through Cairo, she ran across a neo-Buddhist who turned her onto words like inner peace and equilibrium. She was on her way to live with him in Tanzania when she contracted malaria. "But look!" she exclaimed, tossing up her hands. "I wound up here!" As if it were all settled.

The shell collector nursed and listened and made her toast. Every three days she faded into shivering delirium. He knelt by her and trickled seawater over her chest, as Dr. Kabiru had prescribed.

Most days she seemed fine, babbling her secrets. He fell for her, in his own unspoken way. In the lagoon she would call to him and he would swim to her, show her the even stroke he could muster with his sixty-three-year-old arms. In the kitchen he tried making her pancakes and she assured him, giggling, that they were delicious.

And then one midnight she climbed onto him. Before he was fully awake, they had made love. Afterward he heard her crying. Was sex something to cry about? "You miss your kids," he said.

"No." Her face was in the pillow and her words were muffled. "I don't need them anymore. I just need balance. Equilibrium."

"Maybe you miss your family. It's only natural."

She turned to him. "Natural? You don't seem to miss your kid. I've seen those letters he sends. I don't see you sending any back."

"Well he's thirty . . ." he said. "And I didn't run off."

"Didn't run off? You're three trillion miles from home! Some retirement. No fresh water, no friends. Bugs crawling in the bathtub."

He didn't know what to say: What did she want anyhow? He went out collecting.

Tumaini seemed grateful for it, to be in the sea, under the moon, perhaps just to be away from her master's garrulous guest. He unclipped her harness; she nuzzled his calves as he waded. It was a lovely night, a cooling breeze flowing around their bodies, the warmer tidal current running against it, threading between their legs. Tumaini paddled to a rock perch, and he began to roam, stooped, his fingers probing the sand. A marlinspike, a crowned nassa, a broken murex, a lined bullia, small voyagers navigating the current-packed ridges of sand. He admired them, and put them back where he found them. Just before dawn he found two cone shells he couldn't identify, three inches long and audacious, attempting to devour a damselfish they had paralyzed.

14   **WHEN HE RETURNED, HOURS LATER,** the sun was warm on his head and shoulders and he came smiling into the kibanda to find Nancy catatonic on his cot. Her forehead was cold and damp. He rapped his knuckles on her sternum and she did not reflex. Her pulse measured at twenty, then eighteen. He radioed Dr. Kabiru, who motored his launch over the reef and knelt beside her and spoke in her ear. "Bizarre reaction to malaria," the doctor mumbled. "Her heart hardly beats."

The shell collector paced his kibanda, blundered into chairs and tables that had been unmoved for ten years. Finally he knelt on the kitchen floor, not praying so much as buckling. Tumaini, who was agitated and confused, mistook despair for playfulness, and rushed to him, knocking him over. Lying there, on the tile, Tumaini slobbering on his cheek, he felt the cone shell, the snail inching its way, blindly, purposefully, toward the door.

Under a microscope, the shell collector had been told, the teeth of cones look long and sharp, like tiny translucent bayonets, the razor-edged tusks of a miniature ice-devil. The proboscis slips out the siphonal canal, unrolling, the barbed teeth spring forward. In victims the bite causes a spreading insentience, a rising tide of paralysis. First your palm goes horribly cold, then your forearm, then your shoulder. The chill spreads to your chest. You can't swallow, you can't see. You burn. You freeze to death.

"THERE IS NOTHING," Dr. Kabiru said, eyeing the snail, "I can do for this. No antivenom, no fix. I can do nothing." He wrapped Nancy in a blanket and sat by her in a canvas chair and ate a mango with his penknife. The shell collector boiled the cone shell in the chai pot and forked the snail out with a steel needle. He held the shell, 15 fingered its warm pavilion, felt its mineral convolutions.

Ten hours of this vigil, this catatonia, a sunset and bats feeding and the bats gone full-bellied into their caves at dawn and then Nancy came to, suddenly, miraculously, bright-eyed.

"*That*," she announced, sitting up in front of the dumbfounded doctor, "was the most incredible thing ever." Like she had just finished viewing some hypnotic, twelve-hour cartoon. She claimed the sea had turned to ice and snow blew down around her and all of it—the sea, the snowflakes, the white frozen sky—pulsed. "*Pulsed*!" she shouted. "Sssshhh!" she yelled at the doctor, at the stunned shell collector. "It's still pulsing! *Whump! Whump*!"

She was, she exclaimed, cured of malaria, cured of delirium; she was *balanced*. "Surely," the shell collector said, "you're not entirely recovered," but even as he said this he wasn't so sure. She smelled different, like melt-water, like slush, glaciers softening in spring. She spent the morning swimming in the lagoon, squealing and splashing. She ate a tin of peanut butter, practiced high leg kicks on the beach, cooked a feast, swept the kibanda, sang Neil Diamond songs in a high, scratchy voice. The doctor motored off, shaking his head; the shell collector sat on the porch and listened to the palms, the sea beyond them.

That night there was another surprise: she begged to be bitten with a cone again. She promised she'd fly directly home to be with her kids, she'd phone her husband in the morning and plead forgiveness, but first he had to sting her with one of those incredible shells one more time. She was on her knees. She pawed up his shorts. "Please," she begged. She smelled so different.

16   He refused. Exhausted, dazed, he sent her away on a water taxi to Lamu.

THE SURPRISES WEREN'T OVER. The course of his life was diving into its reverse spiral by now, into that dark, whorling aperture. A week after Nancy's recovery, Dr. Kabiru's motor launch again came sputtering over the reef. And behind him were others; the shell collector heard the hulls of four or five dhows come over the coral, heard the splashes as people hopped out to drag the boats ashore. Soon his kibanda was crowded. They stepped on whelks drying on the front step, trod over a pile of chitons by the bathroom. Tumaini retreated under the shell collector's cot, put her muzzle on her paws.

Dr. Kabiru announced that a mwadhini, the mwadhini of Lamu's oldest and largest mosque, was here to visit the shell collector, and with him were the mwadhini's brothers, and his brothers-in-law. The shell collector shook the men's hands as they greeted him, dhow-builders' hands, fishermen's hands.

The doctor explained that the mwadhini's daughter was terribly ill; she was only eight years old and her already malignant malaria had become something altogether more malignant, something the doctor did not recognize. Her skin had gone mustard-seed yellow, she threw up several times a day, her hair fell out. For the past three days she had been delirious, wasted. She tore at her own skin. Her wrists had to be bound to the headboard. These men, the doctor said, wanted the shell collector to give her the same treatment he had given the American woman. He would be paid.

The shell collector felt them crowded into the room, these ocean Muslims in their rustling kanzus and squeaking flip-flops, each stinking of his work—gutted perch, fertilizer, hull-tar—each leaning in to hear his reply.

"This is ridiculous," he said. "She will die. What happened to Nancy was some kind of fluke. It was not a treatment."

"We have tried everything," the doctor said.

"What you ask is impossible," the shell collector repeated. "Worse than impossible. Insane."

There was silence. Finally a voice directly before him spoke, a strident, resonant voice, a voice he heard five times a day as it swung out from loudspeakers over the rooftops of Lamu and summoned people to prayer. "The child's mother," the mwadhini began, "and I, and my brothers, and my brothers' wives, and the whole island, we have prayed for this child. We have prayed for many months. It seems sometimes that we have always prayed for her. And then

AT LOW TIDE, accompanied by an entourage of the mwadhini's brothers, the shell collector waded with Tumaini out onto the reef and began to upturn rocks and probe into the sand beneath, to try to extract a cone. Each time his fingers flurried into loose sand, or into a crab-guarded socket in the coral, a volt of fear would speed down his arm and jangle his fingers. *Conus tessulatus, Conus obscurus, Conus geographus*, who knew what he would find. The waiting proboscis, the poisoned barbs of an expectant switchblade. You spend your life avoiding these things; you end up seeking them out.

He whispered to Tumaini, "We need a small one, the smallest we can," and she seemed to understand, wading with her ribs against his knee, or paddling when it became too deep, but these men leaned in all around him, splashing in their wet kanzus, watching with their dark, redolent attention.

By noon he had one, a tiny tessellated cone he hoped couldn't paralyze a housecat, and he dropped it in a mug with some seawater.

They ferried him to Lamu, to the mwadhini's home, a surfside jumba with marble floors. They led him to the back, up a vermicular staircase, past a tinkling fountain, to the girl's room. He found her hand, her wrist still lashed to the bedpost, and held it. It was small and damp and he could feel the thin fan of her bones through her skin. He poured the mug out into her palm and folded her fingers, one by one, around the snail. It seemed to pulse there, in the delicate vaulting of her hand, like the small dark heart at the center of a songbird. He was able to imagine, in acute detail, the snail's translucent proboscis as it slipped free, the quills of its teeth probing her skin, the venom spilling into her.

"What," he asked into the silence, "is her name?"

FURTHER AMAZEMENT: the girl, whose name was Seema, recovered. Completely. For ten hours she was cold, catatonic. The shell collector spent the night standing in a window, listening to Lamu: donkeys clopping up the street, nightbirds squelching from somewhere in the acacia to his right, hammer strokes on metal, far off, and the surf, washing into the pylons of the docks. He heard the morning prayer sung in the mosques. He began to wonder if he'd been forgotten, if hours ago the girl had passed gently into death and no one had thought to tell him. Perhaps a mob was silently gathering to drag him off and stone him and wouldn't he have deserved every stone?

But then the cooks began whistling and clucking, and the mwadhini, who had squatted by his daughter nightlong, palms up in supplication, hurried past. "Chapatis," he gushed. "She wants chapatis." The mwadhini brought her them himself, cold chapatis slavered with mango jam.

By the following day everyone knew a miracle had occurred in the mwadhini's house. Word spread, like a drifting cloud of coral eggs, spawning, frenzied; it left the island and lived for a while in the daily gossip of coastal Kenyans. The *Daily Nation* ran a back-page story, and KBC ran a minute-long radio spot featuring sound bites from Dr. Kabiru: "I did not know one hundred percent, that it would work, no. But, having extensively researched, I was confident . . ."

Within days the shell collector's kibanda became a kind of pilgrim's destination. At almost any hour, he heard the buzz of motorized dhows, or the oar-knocking of rowboats, as visitors came over the reef into the lagoon. Everyone, it seemed, had a sickness that required remedy. Lepers came, and children with ear infections, a single substantial sentence: *Hi Pop! Things are just fabulous in Michigan! I bet it's sunny in Kenya! Have a wonderful Labor Day! Love you tons!*

This month's letter, however, was different.

"*Dear Pop!*" it read,

> *. . . I've joined the Peace Corps! I'll be working in Uganda for three years! And guess what else? I'm coming to stay with you first! I've read about the miracles you've been working—it's news even here. You got blurbed in* The Humanitarian! *I'm so proud! See you soon!*

24

Six mornings later Josh splashed in on a water taxi. Immediately he wanted to know why more wasn't being done for the sick people clumped in the shade behind the kibanda. "Sweet Jesus!" he exclaimed, slathering suntan lotion over his arms. "These people are *suffering*! These poor orphans!" He crouched over three Kikuyu boys. "Their faces are covered with tiny flies!"

How strange it was to have his son under his roof, to hear him unzip his huge duffel bags, to come across his Schick razor on the sink. Hearing him chide ("You feed your dog *prawns*?"), chug papaya juice, scrub pans, wipe down counters—who was this person in his home? Where had he come from?

The shell collector had always suspected that he did not know his son one whit. Josh had been raised by his mother; as a boy he preferred the baseball diamond to the beach, cooking to conchology. And now he was thirty. He seemed so energetic, so good . . . so stupid. He was like a golden retriever, fetching things, sloppy-tongued, panting, falling over himself to please. He used two days of fresh water giving the Kikuyu boys showers. He spent seventy shillings on a sisal basket that should have cost him seven. He insisted on sending visitors off with care packages: plantains or House of Mangi tea biscuits, wrapped in paper and tied off with yarn.

"You're doing fine, Pop," he announced one evening at the table. He had been there a week. Every night he invited strangers, diseased people, to the dinner table. Tonight it was a paraplegic girl and her mother. Josh spooned chunks of curried potato onto their plates. "You can afford it." The shell collector said nothing. What could he say? Josh shared his blood; this thirty-year-old do-gooder had somehow grown out of him, out of the spirals of his own DNA.

Because he could only take so much of Josh, and because he could not shell for fear of being followed, he began to slip away with Tumaini to walk the shady groves, the sandy plains, the hot, leafless thickets of the island. It was strange moving away from the shore rather than toward it, climbing thin trails, moving inside the ceaseless cicada hum. His shirt was torn by thorns, his skin chewed by insects, his cane struck unidentifiable objects: was that a fencepost? A tree? Soon these walks became shorter; he would hear rustles in the thickets, snakes or wild dogs, perhaps—who knew what awful things bustled in the thickets of that island?—and he'd wave his cane in the air and Tumaini would yelp and they would hurry home.

One day he came across a cone shell in his path, toiling through dust half a kilometer from the sea. *Conus textile*, a common enough

Its columella is mostly straight." The boys stared at him as he read, hummed senseless, joyful songs.

The shell collector heard Josh, one afternoon, reading to them about cones. "The admirable cone is thick and relatively heavy, with a pointed spire. One of the rarest cone shells, it is white, with brown spiral bands."

Gradually, amazingly, after a week of afternoon readings, the boys grew interested. The shell collector would hear them sifting through the banks of shell fragments left by the spring tide. "Bubble shell!" one would shout. "Kafuna found a bubble shell!" They plunged their hands into the rocks and squealed and shouted and dragged shirtfulls of clams up to the kibanda, identifying them with made-up names: "Blue Pretty! Mbaba Chicken Shell!"

One evening the three boys were eating with them at the table, and he listened to them as they shifted and bobbed in their chairs and clacked their silverware against the table edge like drummers. "You boys have been shelling," the shell collector said.

"Kafuna swallowed a butterfly shell!" one of the boys yelled.

The shell collector pressed forward: "Do you know that some of the shells are dangerous, that dangerous things—bad things—live in the water?"

"Bad shells!" one squealed.

"Bad sheelllls!" the others chimed.

Then they were eating, quietly. The shell collector sat, and wondered.

HE TRIED AGAIN, THE NEXT MORNING. Josh was hacking coconuts on the front step. "What if those boys get bored with the beach and go out to the reef? What if they fall into fire coral? What if they step on an urchin?"

"Are you saying I'm not keeping an eye on them?" Josh said.

"I'm saying that they might be looking to get bitten. Those boys came here because they thought I could find some magic shell that will cure people. They're here to get stung by a cone shell."

"You don't have the slightest idea," Josh said, "why those boys are here."

"But you do? You think you've read enough about shells to teach them how to look for cones. You *want* them to find one. You hope they'll find a big cone, get stung, and be cured. Cured of whatever ailment they have. I don't even see anything wrong with them."

"Pop," Josh groaned, "those boys are mentally handicapped. I do *not* think some sea-snail is going to cure them."

29

SO, FEELING VERY OLD, AND VERY BLIND, the shell collector decided to take the boys shelling. He took them out into the lagoon, where the water was flat and warm, wading almost to their chests, and worked alongside them, and did his best to show them which animals were dangerous. "Bad sheellllls!" the boys would scream, and cheered as the shell collector tossed a testy blue crab out, over the reef, into deeper water. Tumaini barked too, and seemed her old self, out there with the boys, in the ocean she loved so dearly.

FINALLY IT WAS NOT ONE OF THE BOYS or some other visitor who was bitten, but Josh. He came dashing along the beach, calling for his father, his face bloodless.

for all the world to peer at: his shell-cluttered kibanda, his pitiful tragedies.

At dusk he rode with them into Lamu. The taxi let them off on a pier and they climbed a hill to town. He heard birds call from the scrub by the road, and from the mango trees that leaned over the path. The air smelled sweet, like cabbage and pineapple. The Jims labored as they walked.

In Lamu the streets were crowded and the street vendors were out, grilling plantains or curried goat over driftwood coals. Pineapples were being sold on sticks, and children moved about yoked with boxes from which they hawked maadazi or chapatis spread with ginger. The Jims and the shell collector bought kebabs and sat in an alley, their backs against a carved wooden door. Before long a passing teenager offered hashish from a water pipe, and the Jims accepted. The shell collector smelled its smoke, sweet and sticky, and heard the water bubble in the pipe.

"Good?" the teenager asked.

"You bet," the Jims coughed. Their speech was slurred.

The shell collector could hear men praying in the mosques, their chants vibrating down the narrow streets. He felt a bit strange, listening to them, as if his head were no longer connected to his body.

"It is Taraweeh," the teenager said. "Tonight Allah determines the course of the world for next year."

"Have some," one of the Jims said, and shoved the pipe in front of the shell collector's face. "More," the other Jim said, and giggled.

The shell collector took the pipe, inhaled.

IT WAS WELL AFTER MIDNIGHT. A crab fisherman in a motorized mtepe was taking them up the archipelago, past banks of mangroves, toward home. The shell collector sat in the bow on a crab trap made from chicken wire and felt the breeze in his face. The boat slowed. "Tokeni," the fisherman said, and the shell collector did, the Jims with him, splashing down from the boat into chest-deep water.

The crab boat motored away and the Jims began murmuring about the phosphorescence, admiring the glowing trails blooming behind each other's bodies as they moved through the water. The shell collector took off his sandals and waded barefoot, down off the sharp spines of coral rock, into the deeper lagoon, feeling the hard furrows of intertidal sand and the occasional mats of algal turf, fibrous and ropy. The feeling of disconnectedness had continued, been amplified by the hashish, and it was easy for him to pretend that his legs were unconnected to his body. He was, it seemed suddenly, floating, rising above the sea, feeling down through the water with impossibly long arms into the turquoise shallows and coral-lined alleys. This small reef: the crabs in their expeditions, the anemones tossing their heads, the blizzards of tiny fish wheeling past, pausing, bursting off . . . he felt it all unfold simply below him. A cowfish, a triggerfish, the harlequin Picasso fish, a drifting sponge—all these lives were being lived out, every day, as they always had been. His senses became supernatural: beyond the breaking combers, the dappled lagoon, he heard terns, and the thrum of insects in the acacias, and the heavy shifting of leaves in avocado trees, the sounding of bats, the dry rasping of bark at the collars of coconut palms, spiky burrs dropping from bushes into hot sand, the smooth

33

the snail brought its foot from the aperture and resumed hauling itself over the sand. The shell collector, using his fingers, followed it for a while, then stood. "Beautiful," he murmured. Beneath his feet the snail kept on, feeling its way forward, dragging the house of its shell, fitting its body to the sand, to the private unlit horizons that whorled all around it.

THE BOY WHO TALKED WITH ANIMALS

by ROALD DAHL

While ROALD DAHL (1916–1990) was most famous for his children's classics, he also wrote darkly imaginative fiction for adults. In "The Boy Who Talked with Animals," the narrator witnesses a strange scene on a Jamaica beach, where a little boy risks his life to save an ancient sea turtle. From the collection The Wonderful World of Henry Sugar, *this simple tale celebtrates the determination of children and the power of imagination.*

NOT SO LONG AGO, I decided to spend a few days in the West Indies. I was to go there for a short holiday. Friends had told me it was marvelous. I would laze around all day long, they said, sunning myself on the silver beaches and swimming in the warm green sea.

I chose Jamaica, and flew direct from London to Kingston. The drive from Kingston airport to my hotel on the north shore took two hours. My room in the hotel had a little balcony, and from there I could step straight down onto the beach. There were tall coconut palms growing all around, and every so often an enormous green nut the size of a football would fall out of the sky and drop with a thud on the sand. It was considered foolish to linger underneath a coconut palm because if one of those landed on your head, it would smash your skull.

The Jamaican girl who came to tidy my room told me that a wealthy American called Mr. Wasserman had met his end in precisely that manner only two months before.

"You're joking," I said to her.

"Not joking!" she cried. "No, *suh*! I sees it happening with my very own eyes!"

"But wasn't there a terrific fuss about it?" I asked.

"They hush it up," she answered darkly. "The hotel folks hush it up and so do the newspaper folks because things like that are very bad for the tourist business."

"And you say you actually saw it happen?"

"I actually saw it happen," she said. "Mr. Wasserman, he's standing right under that very tree over there on the beach. He's got his camera out and he's pointing it at the sunset. It's a red sunset that evening, and very pretty. Then all at once, down comes a big green nut right smack onto the top of his bald head, *wham*! And that," she added with a touch of relish, "is the very last sunset Mr. Wasserman ever did see."

"You mean it killed him instantly?"

"I don't know about *instantly*," she said. "I remember the next thing that happens the camera falls out of his hands onto the sand. Then his arms drop down to his sides and hang there. Then he starts swaying. He sways backward and forward, several times ever so gentle, and I'm standing there watching him, and I says to myself the poor man's gone all dizzy and maybe he's going to faint any moment. Then very very slowly, he keels right over and down he goes."

"Was he dead?"

"Dead as a doornail," she said.

"Good heavens."

"That's right," she said. "It never pays to be standing under a coconut palm when there's a breeze blowing."

"Thank you," I said. "I'll remember that."

On the evening of my second day, I was sitting on my little balcony with a book in my lap and a tall glass of rum punch in my hand. I wasn't reading the book. I was watching a small green lizard stalking another small green lizard on the balcony floor about six feet away. The stalking lizard was coming up on the other one from behind, moving forward very slowly and very cautiously, and when he came within reach, he flicked out a long tongue and touched the other one's tail. The other one jumped round, and the two of them faced each other, motionless, glued to the floor, crouching, staring, and very tense. Then suddenly, they started doing a funny little hopping dance together. They hopped in the air. They hopped backward. They hopped forward. They hopped sideways. They circled one another like two boxers, hopping and prancing and dancing all the time. It was a queer thing to watch, and I guess it was some sort of a courtship ritual they were going through. I kept very still, waiting to see what was going to happen next.

But I never saw what happened next because at that moment I became aware of a great commotion on the beach below. I glanced over and saw a crowd of people clustering around something at the water's edge. There was a narrow

43

"He would right now," the fisherman said, smiling with brilliant white teeth. "He won't ever hurt you when he's in the ocean, but you catch him and pull him ashore and top him up like this, then man alive, you'd better watch out! He'll snap anything that comes in reach!"

"I guess I'd get a bit snappish myself," the woman said, "if I was in his situation."

One idiotic man had found a plank of driftwood on the sand, and he was carrying it toward the turtle. It was a fair-sized plank, about five feet long and maybe an inch thick. He started poking one end of it at the turtle's head.

"I wouldn't do that," the fisherman said. "You'll only make him madder than ever."

When the end of the plank touched the turtle's neck, the great beast whipped around and the mouth opened wide and *snap*, it took the plank in its mouth and bit through it as if it were made of cheese.

"Wow!" they shouted. "Did you see that! I'm glad it wasn't my arm!"

"Leave him alone," the fisherman said. "It don't help to get him all stirred up."

A paunchy man with wide hips and very short hairy legs came up to the fisherman and said, "Listen, feller. I want that shell. I'll buy it from you." And to his plump wife, he said, "You know what I'm going to do, Mildred? I'm going to take that shell home and have it polished by an expert. Then I'm going to place it smack in the center of our living room! Won't that be something?"

"Fantastic," the plump wife said. "Go ahead and buy it, baby."

"Don't worry," he said. "It's mine already." And to the fisherman, he said, "How much for the shell?"

"I already sold him," the fisherman said. "I sold him shell and all."

"Not so fast, feller," the paunchy man said. "I'll bid you higher. Come on. What'd he offer you?"

"No can do," the fisherman said. "I already sold him."

"Who to?" the paunchy man said.

"To the manager."

"What manager?"

"The manager of the hotel."

"Did you hear that?" shouted another man. "He's sold it to the manager of our hotel. And you know what that means? It means turtle soup, that's what it means."

"Right you are! And turtle steak. You ever have turtle steak, Bill?"

"I never have, Jack. But I can't wait."

"A turtle steak's better than a beefsteak if you cook it right. It's more tender and its got one heck of a flavor."

"Listen," the paunchy man said to the fisherman. "I'm not trying to buy the meat. The manager can have the meat. He can have everything that's inside including the teeth and toenails. All I want is the shell."

"And if I know you, baby," his wife said, beaming at him, "you're going to get the shell."

I stood there listening to the conversation of these

human beings. They were discussing the destruction, the consumption and the flavor of a creature who seemed, even when upside down, to be extraordinarily dignified. One thing was certain. He was senior to any of them in age. For probably one hundred and fifty years he had been cruising in the green waters of the West Indies. He was there when George Washington was President of the United States and Napoleon was being clobbered at Waterloo. He would have been a small turtle then, but he was most certainly there.

And now he was here, upside down on the beach, waiting to be translated into soup and steak. He was clearly alarmed by all the noise and shouting around him. His old wrinkled neck was straining out of its shell, and the great head was twisting this way and that as though searching for someone who would explain the reason for all this ill-treatment.

"How are you going to get him up to the hotel?" the paunchy man asked.

"Drag him up the beach with the rope," the fisherman answered. "The staff'll be coming along soon to take him. It's going to need ten men, all pulling at once."

"Hey, listen!" cried a muscular young man. "Why don't *we* drag him up?" The muscular young man was wearing magenta and pea green Bermuda shorts and no shirt. He had an exceptionally hairy chest, and the absence of a shirt was obviously a calculated touch. "What say we do a little work for our supper?" he cried, rippling his muscles. "Come on, fellers! Who's for some exercise?"

"Great idea!" they shouted. "Splendid scheme!"

The men handed their drinks to the women and rushed to catch hold of the rope. They ranged themselves along it as though for a tug-of-war, and the hairy-chested man appointed himself anchorman and captain of the team.

"Come on, now, fellers!" he shouted. "When I say *heave*, then all heave at once, you understand?"

The fisherman didn't like this much. "It's better you leave this job for the hotel," he said.

"Nonsense!" shouted hairy-chest. "*Heave*, boys, *heave*!"

They all heaved. The giant turtle wobbled on its back and nearly toppled over.

"Don't tip him!" yelled the fisherman. "You're going to tip him over if you do that! And if he gets back onto his legs again, he'll escape for sure!"

"Cool it, laddie," said hairy-chest in a patronizing voice. "How can he escape? We've got a rope around him, haven't we?"

"That old turtle will drag the whole lot of you away with him if you give him a chance!" cried the fisherman. "He'll drag you into the ocean, every one of you!"

"*Heave*!" shouted hairy-chest, ignoring the fisherman. "*Heave*, boys, *heave*!"

And now the gigantic turtle began very slowly to slide up the beach toward the hotel, toward the kitchens, toward the place where the big knives were kept. The womenfolk and the older, fatter, less athletic men followed alongside, shouting encouragement.

Several people began shuffling their feet around in the sand. Here and there in the crowd it was possible to sense a slight change of mood, a feeling of uneasiness, a touch even of shame. The boy, who could have been no more than eight or nine years old, had stopped struggling with his father now. The father still held him by the wrist, but he was no longer restraining him.

"Go on!" the boy called out. "Let him go! Undo the rope and let him go!" He stood very small and erect, facing the crowd, his eyes shining like two stars and the wind blowing in his hair. He was magnificent.

"There's nothing we can do, David," the father said gently. "Let's go back."

52   "No!" the boy cried out, and at that moment he suddenly gave a twist and wrenched his wrist free from the father's grip. He was away like a streak, running across the sand toward the giant upturned turtle.

"David!" the father yelled, starting after him. "Stop! Come back!"

The boy dodged and swerved through the crowd like a player running with the ball, and the only person who sprang forward to intercept him was the fisherman. "Don't you go near that turtle, boy!" he shouted as he made a lunge for the swiftly running figure. But the boy dodged round him and kept going. "He'll bite you to pieces!" yelled the fisherman. "Stop, boy! Stop!"

But it was too late to stop him now, and as he came running straight at the turtle's head, the turtle saw him, and the huge upside-down head turned quickly to face him.

The voice of the boy's mother, the stricken, agonized wail of the mother's voice rose up into the evening sky. "*David!*" it cried. "*Oh, David!*" And a moment later, the boy was throwing himself onto his knees in the sand and flinging his arms around the wrinkled old neck and hugging the creature to his chest. The boy's cheek was pressing against the turtle's head, and his lips were moving, whispering soft words that nobody else could hear. The turtle became absolutely still. Even his giant flippers stopped waving in the air.

A great sigh, a long soft sigh of relief went up from the crowd. Many people took a pace or two backward, as though trying perhaps to get a little farther away from something that was beyond their understanding. But the father and mother came forward together and stood about ten feet from their son. 53

"Daddy!" the boy cried out, still caressing the old brown head. "Please do something Daddy! Please make them let him go!"

"Can I be of any help here?" said a man in a white suit who had just come down from the hotel. This, as everyone knew, was Mr. Edwards, the manager. He was a tall, beak-nosed Englishman with a long, pink face. "*What* an extraordinary thing!" he said, looking at the boy and the turtle. "He's lucky he hasn't had his head bitten off." And to the boy, he said, "You'd better come away from there now, sonny. That thing's dangerous."

"I want them to let him go!" cried the boy, still cradling

the head in his arms. "Tell them to let him go."

"You realize he could be killed any moment," the manager said to the boy's father.

"Leave him alone," the father said.

"Rubbish," the manager said. "Go in and grab him. But be quick. And be careful."

"No," the father said.

"What do you mean, no?" said the manager. "These things are lethal! Don't you understand that?"

"Yes," the father said.

"Then for heaven's sake, man, get him away!" cried the manager. "There's going to be a very nasty accident if you don't."

"Who owns it?" the father said. "Who owns the turtle?"

"We do," the manager said. "The hotel has bought it."

"Then do me a favor," the father said. "Let me buy it from you."

The manager looked at the father but said nothing.

"You don't know my son," the father said, speaking quietly. "He'll go crazy if it's taken up to the hotel and slaughtered. He'll become hysterical."

"Just pull him away," the manager said. "And be quick about it."

"He loves animals," the father said. "He really loves them. He communicates with them."

The crowd was silent, trying to hear what was being said. Nobody moved away. They stood as though hypnotized.

"If we let it go," the manager said, "they'll only catch

it again."

"Perhaps they will," the father said. "But those things can swim."

"I know they can swim," the manager said. "They'll catch him all the same. This is a valuable item, you must realize that. The shell alone is worth a lot of money."

"I don't care about the cost," the father said. "Don't worry about that. I want to buy it."

The boy was still kneeling in the sand beside the turtle, caressing its head.

The manager took a handkerchief from his breast pocket and started wiping his fingers. He was not keen to let the turtle go. On the other hand, he didn't want another gruesome accident on his private beach this season. Mr. Wasserman and the coconut, he told himself, had been quite enough for one year, thank you very much.

The father said, "I would deem it a great personal favor, Mr. Edwards, if you would let me buy it. And I promise you won't regret it. I'll make quite sure of that."

The manager's eyebrows went up just a fraction of an inch. He had got the point. He was being offered a bribe. That was a different matter. For a few seconds he went on wiping his hands with the handkerchief. Then he shrugged his shoulders and said, "Well, I suppose if it will make your boy feel any better . . ."

"Thank you," the father said.

"Oh, thank you!" the mother cried. "Thank you so very much!"

"Willy," the manager said, beckoning to the fisherman. The fisherman came forward. He looked thoroughly confused. "I've never seen anything like this before in my whole life," he said. "This old turtle was the fiercest I ever caught! He fought like a devil when we brought him in! It took six of us to land him! That boy's crazy!"

"Yes, I know," the manager said. "But now I want you to let him go."

"Let him go!" the fisherman cried, aghast. "You mustn't ever let this one go, Mr. Edwards! He's broke the record! He's the biggest turtle ever been caught on this island! Easy the biggest! And what about our money?"

"You'll get your money."

"I've got the other five to pay off as well," the fisherman said, pointing down the beach.

About a hundred yards down, on the water's edge, five black-skinned almost naked men were standing beside a second boat. "All six of us are in on this, equal shares," the fisherman went on. "I can't let him go till we got the money."

"I guarantee you'll get it," the manager said. "Isn't that good enough for you?"

"I'll underwrite that guarantee," the father of the boy said, stepping forward. "And there'll be an extra bonus for all six of the fishermen just as long as you let him go at once. I mean immediately, this instant."

The fisherman looked at the father. Then he looked at the manager. "Okay," he said. "If that's the way you want it."

"There's one condition," the father said. "Before you get your money, you must promise you won't go straight out and try to catch him again. Not this evening, anyway. Is that understood?"

"Sure," the fisherman said. "That's a deal." He turned and ran down the beach, calling to the other five fisherman. He shouted something to them we couldn't hear, and in a minute or two, all six of them came back together. Five of them were carrying long thick wooden poles.

The boy was still kneeling beside the turtle's head. "David," the father said to him gently. "It's all right now, David. They're going to let him go."

The boy looked round, but he didn't take his arms from the turtle's neck, and he didn't get up. "When?" he asked.

"Now," the father said. "Right now. So you'd better come away."

"You promise?" the boy said.

"Yes, David, I promise."

The boy withdrew his arms. He got to his feet. He stepped back a few paces.

"Stand back, everyone!" shouted the fisherman called Willy. "Stand right back, everybody, please!"

The crowd moved a few yards up the beach. The tug-of-war men let go of the rope and moved back with the others.

Willy got down on his hands and knees and crept very cautiously up to one side of the turtle. Then he began untying the knot in the rope. He kept well out of the range disappeared in the night."

"You mean the turtle boy?"

"That's him," she said. "His parents is raising the roof and the manager's going mad."

"How long's he been missing?"

"About two hours ago his father found his bed empty. But he could've gone any time in the night I reckon."

"Yes," I said. "He could."

"Everybody in the hotel searching high and low," she said. "And a police car just arrived."

"Maybe he just got up early and went for a climb on the rocks," I said.

Her large, dark, haunted-looking eyes rested a moment on my face, then traveled away. "I do not think so," she said, and out she went.

I slipped on some clothes and hurried down to the beach. On the beach itself, two native policemen in khaki uniforms were standing with Mr. Edwards, the manager. Mr. Edwards was doing the talking. The policemen were listening patiently. In the distance, at both ends of the beach, I could see small groups of people, hotel servants as well as hotel guests, spreading out and heading for the rocks. The morning was beautiful. The sky was smoke blue, faintly glazed with yellow. The sun was up and making diamonds all over the smooth sea. And Mr. Edwards was talking loudly to the two native policemen, and waving his arms.

I wanted to help. What should I do? Which way should

I go? It would be pointless simply to follow the others. So I just kept walking toward Mr. Edwards.

About then, I saw the fishing boat. The long wooden canoe with a single mast and a flapping brown sail was still some way out to sea, but it was heading for the beach. The two natives aboard, one at either end, were paddling hard. They were paddling very hard. The paddles rose and fell at such a terrific speed they might have been in a race. I stopped and watched them. Why the great rush to reach the shore? Quite obviously they had something to tell. I kept my eyes on the boat. Over to my left, I could hear Mr. Edwards saying to the two policemen. "It is perfectly ridiculous. I can't have people disappearing just like that from the hotel. You'd better find him fast, you understand me? He's either wandered off somewhere and got lost or he's been kidnapped. Either way, it's the responsibility of the police. . . ."

The fishing boat skimmed over the sea and came gliding up onto the sand at the water's edge. Both men dropped their paddles and jumped out. They started running up the beach. I recognized the one in front as Willy. When he caught sight of the manager and the two policemen, he made straight for them.

"Hey, Mr. Edwards!" Willy called out. "We just seen a crazy thing!"

The manager stiffened and jerked back his neck. The two policemen remained impassive. They were used to excitable people. They met them every day.

61

"We never *stop* calling out, man!" Willy cried. "As soon as the boy sees us and we're not trying to creep up on them any longer, then we start yelling. We yell everything under the sun at that boy to try and get him aboard. 'Hey boy!' I yell at him. 'You come on back with us! We'll give you a lift home! That ain't no good what you're doing there, boy! Jump off and swim while you got the chance and we'll pick you up! Go on, boy, jump! Your mammy must be waiting for you at home, boy, so why don't you come on in with us?' And once I shouted at him, 'Listen boy! We're gonna make you a promise! We promise not to catch that old turtle if you come with us!'"

"Did he answer you at all?" the manager asked.

64   "He never even looks round!" Willy said. "He sits high up on that shell and he's sort of rocking backward and forward with his body just like he's urging the old turtle to go faster and faster! You're gonna lose that little boy, Mr. Edwards, unless someone gets out there real quick and grabs him away!"

The manager's normally pink face had turned white as paper. "Which way were they heading?" he asked sharply.

"North," Willy answered. "Almost due north."

"Right!" the manager said. "We'll take the speedboat! I want you with us, Willy. And you, Tom."

The manager, the two policemen and the two fishermen ran down to where the boat that was used for water skiing lay beached on the sand. They pushed the boat out, and even the manager lent a hand, wading up to his knees in his well-pressed white trousers. Then they all climbed in.

I watched them go zooming off.

Two hours later, I watched them coming back. They had seen nothing.

All through that day, speedboats and yachts from other hotels along the coast searched the ocean. In the afternoon, the boy's father hired a helicopter. He rode in it himself, and they were up there three hours. They found no trace of the turtle or the boy.

For a week, the search went on, but with no result.

And now, nearly a year has gone by since it happened. In that time, there has been only one significant bit of news. A party of Americans, out from Nassau in the Bahamas, were deep-sea fishing off a large island called Eleuthera. There are literally thousands of coral reefs and small uninhabited islands in this area, and upon one of these tiny islands, the captain of the yacht saw through his binoculars the figure of a small person. There was a sandy beach on the islands, and the small person was walking on the beach. The binoculars were passed around, and everyone who looked through them agreed that it was a child of some sort. There was, of course, a lot of excitement on board, and the fishing lines were quickly reeled in. The captain steered the yacht straight for the island. When they were half a mile off, they were able, through the binoculars, to see clearly that the figure on the beach was a boy, and although sunburned, he was almost certainly white-skinned, not a native. At that point, the watchers on the yacht also spotted what looked like a giant turtle on the sand near the boy. What happened next happened very quickly. The boy, who had probably caught sight of the approaching yacht, jumped on the turtle's back, and the huge creature entered the water and swam at great speed around the island and out of sight. The yacht searched for two hours, but nothing more was seen either of the boy or the turtle.

There is no reason to disbelieve this report. There were five people on the yacht. Four of them were Americans and the captain was a Bahamian from Nassau. All of them in turn saw the boy and the turtle through the binoculars.

To reach Eleuthera Island from Jamaica by sea, one must first travel northeast for two hundred and fifty miles and pass through the Windward Passage between Cuba and Haiti. Then one must go north-northwest for a further three hundred miles at least. This is a total distance of five hundred and fifty miles, which is a very long journey for a small boy to make on the shell of a giant turtle.

Who knows what to think of all of this?

One day, perhaps, he will come back, though I personally doubt it. I have a feeling he's quite happy where he is.

LIVE LIFE KING-SIZED *by* HESTER KAPLAN

HESTER KAPLAN (b. 1959), who lives in Rhode Island, has said that a brochure for a tropical resort inspired her to write this story, a luminescent tale of inheritance and sacrifice. Her collection of short stories, The Edge of Marriage, *received a Flannery O'Connor Prize for Short Fiction in 1999.*

LATE IN THE SUMMER OF 1993, a hurricane with the gentle name of Tess smashed everything I had into a million pieces. From a window in the cement cooling house where I waited out the storm, I watched the wind suck all the water from the pool, lift the thatch roof from the tiki hut, and detonate the last of the beach chairs. Square by square, the dining room patio was untiled, and just before Tess changed course, a single wave plucked out the entire length of dock.

Hours earlier, my staff had left for the main island, cramming themselves into four tiny boats, which seemed more dangerous than any hurricane. I'd told them to take what food they wanted from the kitchen freezers—we'd lose power and it would all spoil—but they still hid it in their bags and under straw hats. They yelled that I was a crazy yellow-haired man to stare a hurricane in the eye. She will think you're making fun of death, they warned, shielding themselves she looked obscene with health next to him.

I had checked her in the evening before—they were Cecelia and Henry Blaze, from just outside Boston. Henry, she'd explained while signing the registration slip with her own gold-capped pen, didn't travel well; they would skip dinner. Under the bougainvillea'd portico, I could just make out his bent shape among the bags Jono was piling into the cart that would buzz them to their cabana. They were staying for three weeks, Cecelia reminded me as she slipped her pen back in her purse, and she hoped the weather would hold. She was in her mid-fifties, and I could see that she'd been pretty once, but over-efficiency and some sadness had taken it out of her. Distracted by the noise in the kitchen at that moment, I didn't think about the Blazes again.

Now, as Henry Blaze creaked himself onto one of the pool chairs, I anxiously waited for leisure to return poolside, but I saw from the looks on the faces of the other guests that it wasn't going to come back so easily. No one wants to see reality on vacation, and this was an awful lot of reality on such a bright day. If my first thought about Henry Blaze was to get him the hell out of here, my second was, is this death making fun back at me? Tess had nearly wiped me out. After everything, I was not going to let a dead man kill me now.

BEFORE DINNER THAT EVENING, I searched for my one remaining pair of long white pants and linen shirt. My cabana—bedroom, sitting room, bathroom—was the only place that still looked like the hurricane had just blown through. I had replaced the broken windows, but the roof continued to leak and the floor buckled. My bed was unmade—I didn't allow housekeeping in here—the unused half covered with papers, clothes, music tapes I ordered through the mail, a plate and coffee cup from breakfast.

Some views might be bigger, but I liked the one from my bedroom the best. A blue lozenge of water glimmered at the end of a tunnel of sea grape leaves, a less-is-more equation of beauty, and for a seductive second I was stuck on it. I heard calm among the guests, the routine clink of drinks being served on the dining room patio, the two young men I'd hired the week before joking as they put away beach equipment. I had a startling flash of Blaze among the trees, and the possibility that I might lose all this—and then where would I go?—hit me for the second time that day. The outside world seemed tremulous, and without borders.

It was too late to iron my shirt once I found it, so I tried to smooth out the wrinkles as I walked to the dining room, where the guests were already attempting to outdo each other with descriptions of the sunset. Relieved that Blaze was not around—I assumed he was eating in his cabana and I was spared for the moment—I entered the room as the perfectly confident proprietor.

The book group, shiny in sundresses, ordered a bottle of wine as I stood by their table, hands behind my back. I inhaled their smells, which made me a little forgetful as I leaned over glossy shoulders to pour. One of the women had a wonderful, shocked laugh and a head of spiky hair I liked. At another table, the Jensens already had the waiters in a state of mild panic, which seemed to give Bob Jensen a feeling of great power. I'd seen this type before, entitled not by the having of money but simply by the spending of it. Still, I couldn't deny that the table exuded a kind of welcome, affluent energy.

"How are you all doing?" I said, placing my hand on Jensen's with his tray of melting ice cream for the Jensens.

"Here, let me help you," I offered, and bent down next to Cecelia, who was now kneeling, her skin pale against the red tiles. Her skirt was unwrapped up the length of a freckled thigh, revealing sad white underpants.

"I have it," she said, but continued to pull uselessly at the tubing.

A nervous odor rose off Blaze. I was now almost cheek to cheek with his wife, and a little desperate. "The goddamn thing's taped up," I said.

Cecelia shot me a look of disapproval. She flipped her skirt shut, sat back, and with what seemed like total, prideful indifference tossed the problem to me; her husband was going to die in *my* dining room. Blaze shifted to the right then, and with a small, almost dainty cough, threw up his dinner. A moment later, he took a full, wheezeless sigh while a splatter slid off his square knees onto the floor.

I stood too fast and motioned for my staff to come clean up; suddenly they were blind to me, and I was dizzy.

"Goddamn it!" Blaze said. For the first time we looked directly at each other, and I saw from his eyes that he wasn't really old at all. I could have felt sorry for him then—all this misery in a man just sixty—but I was even less forgiving than earlier that he'd chosen my place for this freak show of his.

After some cleaning up, Cecelia slouched her husband out of the room. I assured the book group that Blaze would be fine, though I could seem them rallying as concerned women now and not vacationers. I sent Jensen another beer, which he received with a verdictless shrug, and I turned on the ceiling fan to blow the death smell of Henry Blaze out to sea.

Later, the book club played poker and scattered plastic chips on the patio floor, their tone a little off, like people having a good time at a wake. I heard the clatter of bikes and mopeds behind the kitchen as the staff heckled their way home. In the front office, I checked the computer, as I did every night now, to see if new reservations had come in since I'd last looked. There was only one, and that not yet confirmed. I put my head in my hands.

"Jesus H., that was some scene with the old man tonight," Bob Jensen said, peering into the office and startling me. "Disturbing you?"

"Disturbing me? No, just shutting up for the night," I said. I wanted to tell him not to stroll where he wasn't welcome, and I knew by the way he was hanging around that I'd have to open the bar and give the guy a drink on the house pretty soon. I turned out the office light.

"So, I thought he was going to die right there," Jensen continued as we walked outside. He shivered for a second in the heat. "You know the noise he made, like a spoon went down his garbage disposal. Kind of freaked my wife and kids. Let's not even talk about the spewing."

"Let me get you a drink, Mr. Jensen," I said, and led him to the dark tiki bar. He hoisted himself onto a stool and told me what a nice place I had. With his broad back half turned to me, he watched the anoles skitter by the pool lights and sipped his Cuba Libre.

"Okay, what I'm wondering," he said, "is maybe the old guy could eat earlier or later or in his cabana or something. You don't think I'm being hard, do you?" Jensen said, his voice falsely sappy.

Mr. Thierry. I take it your guests didn't like my performance at dinner," he said. "But now Cecelia has those nice bookish women to talk to because of me. They've adopted her, I think."

"Please, Mr. Blaze." My impatience surprised him only a little—I could tell he enjoyed revving people up and letting them whirl uselessly. "I'm trying to hold on to this place, and I do know I can't afford to have guests pull out now because they're unhappy or decide to go somewhere else next year, for whatever reason. I'm not sure this is the best place for you to be."

"You mean I'm not an asset." Blaze countered my ugly lack of sympathy and squinted at the water again. "Your guests are too uptight."

"You have to understand my position." The truth was, I could only ask him to leave; I couldn't actually force him out.

"I understand your position well enough, Mr. Thierry. Now look at mine."

Blaze was not wearing a shirt, and I saw how trim and beautiful his body must have been before he got sick, before he became distended, toxic and puffy in some places, deflated in others. A bracelet of thin black leather circled his wrist, a strange touch on such a pale American. I was repulsed by his body, and when I turned away, I saw what he had been looking at so intently while we had talked. On the large sandbar, not far offshore, the honeymooners from Philadelphia were bare-chested, their faces pressed tightly together. She was lying on top of him, while his hands circled the sides of her breasts and then the rise of her ass. Their bright orange kayaks sat nose first on the sand, the single palm tree fanning a wasted shade over them.

"Not exactly private, is it?" Blaze laughed, a little wistfully, I thought.

I sat down on the low wall. My eyes adjusted to the darkness of the room behind Blaze, and to the squadrons of pill bottles and inhalers on the wicker bureau. Last night's oxygen dolly stood by the unmade bed. For the first time, it occurred to me that Blaze might have AIDS, with his collection of mismatched and terrible ravages. Our island is an oil well of pleasure, and I'd seen enough sick people standing in cool and furtive doorways in town to know this particular disease.

"Why did you come here?" I asked.

"You think I singled you out."

"Seems that way," I said. "There are a million islands, Mr. Blaze. You could have gone to Club Med even—they would have given you your own bikinied nurses round the clock."

"Not my thing, Mr. Thierry." Blaze looked up at the sky. "I can see the hurricane did a lot of damage here. This was the most beautiful spot on earth, and I've been to some pretty spectacular places all over the world. I remember you. I remember your mother too."

"You've been here before?" I asked, skeptically.

"Several times, actually—last with my first wife, years and years ago. You must have been around thirteen then, miserable and pimply, performing an impressive repertoire of antisocial activities for the guests. You once stood on a rock and peed into the water while we were having dinner in the dining room. Your mother tried to distract us with shrimp cocktail. Jumbo shrimp, she kept saying, look at the size of their tails. All I saw was your skinny ass in the sunset. Still, I always thought it must have been paradise for you, growing up on this island. And now look at you—all business and good interpersonal skills to boot."

There were times I forgot how much I once hated this place, how I couldn't wait to get away. Despairingly fatherless, I had searched among each season's new arrivals for possible candidates. My mother gave me nothing to go on, though. She claimed to know little about who he was. Not because he'd knocked her up and disappeared, or was some married mystery, I was meant to understand, but because that's how she'd wanted it. Mother and child only, the picture of paradise. I was fathered by some resort guest who'd been turned on by my mother's independence and sharp business sense, her long toes, tanned face, and light eyes, the skittery sounds at night, this place so far from his home, the erotic heat in the dark. All she might have had of him was a credit card receipt in her files.

"Why did you come back?" I asked.

"I heard you were hurting for business. I thought I'd help you out a little."

"But I don't think that's what you're doing," I said. "You are definitely not good for business."

"I want to die here, Mr. Thierry," Blaze said, sounding as tired as he looked all of a sudden. "I was hoping you might be sympathetic."

REMOVED AND UP IN HIS WINDY CABANA on the bluff, Blaze stayed away from the other guests, and I had Tom take him his meals. With him out of my sight, I even allowed myself to feel hopeful and hear the hymn bounce off the bluebitch stone and pool's surface again. The Jensen kids napped by the pool. A man, still laughing, had to be brought back off the water when the breeze died on his windsurfer. The honeymooners slept past lunch, other guests settled into their own muted routines, while I willingly busied myself with work, the supplying of other people's pleasure. Cecelia Blaze had been encircled by the book group—they seemed a useful novelty to each other—and her appearance each morning was good news to me and a reminder that three weeks would go by quickly. Blaze would leave, sick but alive, as he had come.

So perhaps it was some blind gratitude, finally, or simply curiosity during a hopeful moment, but I decided to deliver Blaze's lunch myself one noon. Motionless and drained in the shadows indoors, he did not seem surprised to see me, though it had been days. He tentatively examined the tray with his head drawn back, as though the fish might jump up and bite him. I understood then that for someone as sick and weak as he was, the wrong food, wind, breath, dose could easily kill him.

He'd eaten some bad meat in Poona once and had nearly died from it. "My stomach ulcerated, I shit blood," he explained. He took a bite of fruit—he was not starving himself—which he chewed with his front teeth. "You don't know where Poona is, do you, Kip?"

"I haven't done a whole lot of traveling," I said. "Look, I wanted to let you know I appreciate—"

"Northern India. That's your geography lesson for today," Blaze interrupted. Did I know he was the largest importer of Indian movies to the United States? The demand was voracious, he explained, not to be believed, and then he pushed away his plate and could barely keep his eyes open long enough to see me leave. When I delivered his dinner, he was in the same place I'd left him earlier, though this time he didn't talk. His lips were chalky from something Cecelia had buttons on her shirt, her face pale from what she'd obviously just heard him say. She sat in one of the wicker chairs and crossed her legs.

"Don't be such a priss," Blaze said to her, having regained full breath now. He was unkind, she was long-suffering; they seemed to accept their complicity in the situation.

"He was telling me about some of his trips," I said.

"I'm sure he was." She nodded. "Did he tell you how he once forgot to walk clockwise around a Buddhist shrine?" She began to laugh, and pulled her knees up girlishly. "They nearly arrested him. Oh, I don't know, it just seems like the strangest thing to me."

"Cece," Blaze said as though he'd been trying to get her to understand forever, "it is so much more than that."

Her face suddenly tightened as she considered him. Was she picturing at that moment her husband bent over another man, thrusting with passion? Was she wondering where his tongue and mouth had been? He must have also slept years of nights in bed with her, the comforter over them with reassuring weight, the dry kiss on the lips equally reassuring. My husband is not queer, she would tell herself, he does not have sex with men, because he is my husband. She wasn't going to indulge or spare him now—his dying was killing her too, after all. She fiddled with her hair while her eyes watered; the love of her life was retreating, and he didn't want her to come along.

THAT EVENING, still distracted from the morning's scene with the Blazes, I wandered out onto the patio. The book group, having splintered during their week, was back together for a last dinner, looking forced and tired. The spiky-haired woman touched my hand as I walked by—too little, too late, too difficult, I thought—but she only wanted me to see to something.

"Look," she said, and nodded toward the sandbar where Blaze and I had seen the half-naked honeymooners days earlier. I offered a Deserted Island Evening package—wine and lobster at sunset on the tiny island—for an extra fee. It had been my mother's idea early on, an appreciation of the romantic streak in others. At most, there had only been a few takers a season. "God, it's wonderful to see them out together," she sighed.

At the edge of the sandbar, one of the beach boys was helping Cecelia step out of the dinghy. In the evening light, her turquoise dress was diaphanous and slinked around her ankles. Blaze was hunched and uncertain as he lifted his knobby leg to climb out of the boat, one hand heavy on the boy's shoulder. He had not been farther than the terrace of his own cabana in almost a week, and this vastness must have startled him.

Cecelia smoothed a blanket on the sand as the boy left in the boat and Blaze sat down next to her. What a joke to offer up this sandbar as deserted. When you were on it, it felt alone and tiny and the single palm seemed enormous, but from the height of the patio—and from Blaze's terrace, as I had seen—it was a theater stage on which to act out this peculiar marriage. Cecelia's adjustment of her dress, Blaze's shift to one side as he removed something sharp from under himself, the splash as she clumsily poured wine—these were larger than life, lit up for all to see. Blaze had to know this.

We saw how Cecelia wanted to kiss her husband, so when he offered only a cheek, she forcefully took his face in her hands and pulled him toward her, pressing her mouth against his. No one spoke,

I stared at Jensen with obvious contempt while he considered whether or not to hit me. Finally he jumped out of the boat, brushing his shoulder against mine.

"Can you sit?" he yelled at Blaze, as though he were deaf.

Blaze narrowed his eyes even further. "What do you think?"

Jensen and I managed to haul Blaze into the dinghy and lean him against his wife. A small crowd had gathered on the beach, and then, as we were lifting him from the boat, Blaze slipped away from us like a hooked but determined fish. Cecelia and the other gasped, while I wanted to throw my head back and howl with laughter, fall to my knees while the tears streamed down my cheeks. My hands went weak, my bowels and stomach quivered, and Blaze sank fast and helplessly in the shallows. It was where he wanted to be, after all. I should just let him go.

But I grabbed him instead. Jensen was stunned, and Blaze was an even more impossible weight now. His eyes were closed as though he had decided to pass calmly through this humiliation and his failure. Someone had wheeled one of the wooden beach chairs down to the water's edge, and we managed to lay Blaze on it. His dripping clothes hung on the distorted angles of his body, making him look even worse than before. Jensen left, calling to his kids, who were gawking over the patio railing, as though he hadn't seen them in weeks. People flitted around us for a few seconds, while Cecelia sat on the end of the chair and stared out.

"I need to stay here for a minute," Blaze announced.

"I'm going to get you a blanket, a sweater, something," Cecelia said numbly. She stood and walked away.

"She's weaving—it's the wine." Blaze watched her go and then pulled a pack of still-dry cigarettes from his shirt pocket. "Have a lighter, Thierry?"

"Jesus Christ," I said, and lit his cigarette. "You're smoking?"

"Yes." He took a defiantly deep inhalation and looked pleased with himself. "Live life king-sized."

"What's that supposed to mean?"

"Something I liked in an Indian movie, *The Eighth Moon*. Seen it? A real blockbuster," he said. "Everything's about smoking in that country. The prince has just routed a coup, killed a few hundred ingrates, and so he pulls out a cigarette and lights up. 'Live life king-sized,' he declares. It sounded right."

I sat on the end of the chair where Cecelia had been. Blaze's ankle tapped at my thigh as he dragged on his cigarette.

"This outing tonight was my idea," he said, "so don't blame Cecelia. People say she's too stiff, but that's not really true. I think I didn't give her enough time when I was living—not dying, that is— but I love her. Your little island"—he waved his cigarette toward the sandbar—"seemed like it might be the right way to show her." Blaze laughed and pulled himself higher on the chair. "I have no energy to explain anything anymore, Thierry—my disease, my life, my unnatural passions, as it were. I want to die. Seems I'm not having much luck, though."

"It's a little hard to drown yourself in less than a foot of water." I turned around to look at him. "*You* live life king-sized, Blaze. My business is going under."

"Don't be such a pessimist. It shows a great lack of imagination."

"So what if I lose this place," I said, ignoring him. "I can go somewhere else."

music to watch the women bent and swaying over counters, sweat on the backs of their thick necks, feet slipped out of shoes. I had known them forever and so I was still paying them with what little I had left, but there was almost no work to do; they were playing cards, sucking on toothpicks, talking. As I watched, I remembered how once one of the staff had come trembling to me. She swore she'd just seen her long-dead father leaning against the kitchen's back door, smoking and waiting for her to get off work, and she wanted me to shoo him away, which I pretended to do. Now I felt those eyes and a hot breath in the shade and left quickly.

That evening Tom told me the Blazes were waiting for me on the patio. Cecelia was wearing an alarmingly bright dress, huge yellow daisies with blue centers, an ugly island design my mother used to wear on Saturday nights. Henry, in a chair next to her, wasn't eating that day, she told me. First fasting, then a sunset and an enema before bed.

"Like scrubbing the ring off a bathtub," Blaze said. He looked sicker, but also strangely expectant for someone who couldn't expect much of anything anymore. "Has to be done every once in a while so the water's clean. Give it to him, Cece."

"What's this?" I asked, and took the piece of paper Cecelia held out to me. There were fifteen names on the list, all Indian, from what I could tell.

"I've invited my friends, just like I told you I would," Blaze said. "You got a few empty rooms at the moment, am I right?"

"A few," I said weakly. I needed to sit down but leaned heavily against the patio railing, my back to the water.

"Some of them won't be able to come on such short notice, of course," Cecelia said, energized by her sudden usefulness to her husband, even in this deranged task. I couldn't bring myself to look at her, to see what she might or might not understand. "They're Henry's friends, really. You know he was up late last night trying to arrange this over the phone."

"Not easy." Blaze said. "But believe me, I've arranged much more complicated deals than this one. It didn't take much convincing; I offered something for nothing. Most people are pigs." Cecelia laughed at this, and looked a little surprised at her gaiety. Blaze gave her a puzzled look.

"All these people are coming here," I said to Blaze. "Do I have that right?"

"You didn't think I was serious, did you? I can see it in your face," he said. "But a deal is a deal."

Cecelia ignored her husband, as I'd seen her do so many times before. "He's decided he wants them to be here when he dies. They love him." She slapped her hand over her mouth. The way the lowering sun caught in her eyes, I didn't know if she was horrified, thrilled, or both.

BLAZE DELIVERED ON HIS PROMISE, and over the next few days, fourteen of his friends came to my island. Each arrival was another weight for me, more evidence of a debt I was expected to pay back. As a group, though, these people brought with them an attractive, buoyant life I'd never seen before, a new hymn that I sometimes found myself swaying to. They enthusiastically loved the place and wandered noisily into the dining room at the last minute and stayed for hours, swam at night, slept most of the morning, talked endlessly to me about the island, the birds, and Blaze.

Sanjiv Bhargava, a large and slickly confident man, was Blaze's closest friend among the group, and often sought me out with earnest questions about natural history and my childhood on the island. Three of the guests brought wives, who rubbed oil on their dark skin for hours and melted into each other around the pool. Cecelia looked uncomfortable around them at first, so stiff, with her mouth mimicking the curve of her arching hairline. She startled at their hands resting on her arms, her knees, the way they included her.

Blaze sat kinglike in the middle, but shut out the sudden activity that now swirled around him. Watching him from the window in the main house that overlooked the pool, I was the only one who noticed that he was in deeper trouble now, that his face contorted with spasms and he fell asleep with his mouth open. In the space of only a few days his chest had collapsed, so that a hollow preceded him, sat on his lap, sucked up his words. These friends of his—fully paid-for and loving their mid-winter luck—swam and teased, but they never tuned their heads to check on him, as though he should be my responsibility now.

One morning Blaze's friends left him while they went down to the beach. Squinting uncomfortably, Blaze sat in the direct early heat but appeared not to have the strength to move himself. Finally, when I could no longer stand to see him purpling and swelling in the sun, I came out of the main house and moved his chair into the shade. I was quick to hurry away.

"No, don't go yet," Blaze said, and caught my arm. "Tell me, Thierry, how does my future look these days?" The strength of his voice still surprised me.

"I don't know about your future," I stalled. I saw Cecelia and Blaze's friends circling past around a pair of sailboats on the beach, considering their next activity. "What do your doctors say?"

Blaze laughed. "You want to know what my doctors say? All right," he said. "They are institutionally optimistic. They should all be forced to wear buttons that say 'Be hopeful,' and at night they should have to lay the buttons down next to their alarm clocks so they will be the first thing they see when they wake up, even before they take a leak. But enough already with the optimism, don't you think? It doesn't do me any good." He nodded toward the beach, his wife and friends, and his eyes teared. "Anyway, I've arranged everything. My friends will be back next year with their big brown families and business partners and silent, glaring grandmas who don't speak English—all on my nickel. So you'll be okay, Thierry, don't worry. Now put me back in the sun."

My mother called a little later. Cold as hell in New York, she said hoarsely, as though clots of snow were lodged in her throat. She'd just walked back from the museum and was thinking of buying a pair of snow pants like the ones all the kids had. Since my mother had left this island—ambivalent, but more than ready—she had gorged herself on choice.

"I hear you're running a leper colony down there, you've got people throwing up in the dining room," she said. Her friend at Columbus Travel (sister of the reservationist who'd booked the Jensen family) had called to report. Several others had apparently done the same.

"Yes, a leper colony. We've got body parts all over the place, but we can fit fifteen people in one bed." I wondered what she would make of Blaze, still alone and in the sun—if she would recognize him through his disease as someone from another time in her life.

"You can joke if you want," my mother said. "But if *I've* heard it, imagine how many other people have too. Word of mouth can kill your business in a second, Kip. I'm absolutely serious, it doesn't take much."

"I know."

My mother sighed. "This man Jensen claims he's going to report you—to whom and for what, who knows, but he's telling everyone. At the very least, he's looking for a full refund. There's an asshole in every crowd, remember that—you have to give him the Asshole Special, even if it means crawling to do it to save the business." My mother stopped short. Giving me advice made her uncomfortable, since she'd never gotten or asked for any herself. I knew she'd moved over to the window and was thinking, with enormous, familiar regret, how slowly the traffic below her was moving. "Are you in trouble, Kip?"

From my window, I saw one of Tom's young nephews creep past Blaze's chair and slip into the pool. My staff and their kids hissed at him excitedly to get out of the pool, which was off-limits, but he dunked and came up sputtering, his eyes completely round as he rubbed his hands across his nipples, electrifying himself. Blaze stirred in his chair and smiled. Some muted chaos had taken over.

"I am," I told my mother just before we hung up.

Blaze threw something into the pool then, a shell he'd had in his curled hand as though he'd been waiting for this, and the children dove for it. The commotion and the splashes that landed on his hot face pleased him, but his body seized with pain in retaliation. I thought he might die then, even if he lived for weeks or months, he was so close. Would it be so bad simply to help along the inevitable now? I wondered, for the briefest moment, how it might happen. I could slip him an overdose in a glass of papaya juice, which he would eagerly accept. In the privacy of his cabana, I could cover his face with a damp towel and look away. But I'd heard the body struggled violently on its own at the end—a thought that made me sick to my stomach—and who was I to hold this man down?

AS I DROVE SANJIV INTO TOWN ONE MORNING, he told me that he owned a chain of twelve shoe stores in New Jersey and had at least one relative working in every shop. Earlier he had asked if he could use the kitchen that night—a meal for Henry was what he had in mind—and if I'd show him where he could buy some of the ingredients he needed.

"Full compliance with your requirements and schedule," he had said formally, meaning that this was to take place after the regular dinner for the few other guests and he would pay for everything. He toured the kitchen, walking regally among the staff with their tilted stares and white aprons, found it missing what he needed, hiked up his perfectly pressed black linen shorts and gave me a broad smile.

I parked the car off the main street, pointed out a few places he might try—though the town was a tourist rip-off and I didn't think he'd have much luck—and told him I'd meet him in the bar across from the post office. I hadn't been in Sportman's in months, since before the season began. The place was empty, and I sat at the bar. I made conversation with Louis, the owner, whom I'd known for years, a guy who had come to the island after college and never left. Occasionally, he'd show up for dinner with one of his girlfriends and drive home drunk, his hand probably already between her legs.

"Hey, I hear you have some weird shit happening over at your place," Louis said in a conspiratorial whisper, though nothing on the island was secret. "Business sucks and you got all these Indians, for one thing. And a guy died?"

"Not that I know of," I said.

"That's not what I heard." Louis looked up at the planked ceiling, fingered a faded shell necklace around his neck. His face was wrinkled and a little vexed. I wondered if all of us island boys seemed alike, boyish and stunted. We were single and childless and might always be. "He died in the pool or something, right?"

Sanjiv walked in just then and put his heavy plastic bags down by the door as if they contained the most fragile flowers. He removed a thin, honey-colored wallet from his back pocket, placed it on the bar, and sat down next to me. It was unusually hot in town that day, and Sanjiv drank his beer in several gulps. He ordered another one, which he rested between his large hands, tapping the glass with his rings.

"Much better," Sanjiv said. "Now we can talk, Mr. Thierry."

"Find what you were looking for?" I asked.

"Surprisingly, yes. Completely successful." He named a few stores. "And I poked around the video shop here as well, to see what's what in a place like this. Large porno section, one might be surprised to know."

"It can get pretty quiet around here," I said, and Louis smirked. "Long hot winters. Long hot summers, long hot in-betweens."

Sanjiv considered this, sipped his beer slowly, and smiled condescendingly at Louis, who got the hint and backed away. "I will have to tell Henry he is well represented. It will give him much pleasure to know that he has reached even such a place as this."

"Blaze is into porno?"

"Well he imports it, of course. You have to these days to make any money. It is a small part of his business, in fact, but a most lucrative one. He doesn't approve of the stuff."

"Art films, he told me, epics, that sort of thing," I said. "Blockbusters. *The Eighth Moon.*"

"You know that one? Ah, Henry. He's a dealmaker, an orchestrator. I am aware of all his business dealings." Sanjiv laughed. His accent was subtle and covered his words in silk. "You wouldn't think Mrs. Blaze would approve either, would you? And she doesn't, of course." He turned to face me and winked. "She pretends not to know—that and other things. It is a complicated thing, very sad, all of this, AIDS now. We have been lovers, Henry and I, for many years."

We turned back to our beers for a minute, and I felt an enormous pressure to say something, my own confession. "He wants me to help him die. He said he'd bring you here in return."

"Yes, I know that. Henry keeps a promise." Sanjiv nodded, his eyes tearing. "We're all here to say goodbye. He doesn't look good, I agree, and I imagine he will die on this island." He took a sip of his beer. "Henry has told me about you, Mr. Thierry, that he has known you since you were a little boy, and now he will save your island for you. You're a fine businessman, a proprietor, and this is a wonderful place; you'll make a good decision about things," he said knowingly.

"Jesus, killing a man is not a business deal," I said angrily.

Sanjiv shook his head. "No, of course it isn't. It was never meant to be. I love him very much, and I will be sad to see him go, but

I WAS UP EARLIER THAN ANYONE ELSE the next morning, and wandered around my island, drawn finally to the path that led to the Blazes'. At the turn of the bluff, I looked up at their cabana, which had taken a particularly hard beating in the hurricane. I'd rebuilt the pointed roof overhang myself out of aged purple heartwood, which now gleamed with its oily veins. But some angles, I realized that morning, would never be fully realigned, and hints of splinter and tarnish were visible everywhere. Up on the stone terrace, I looked into the cabana and saw the single sleeping, sheeted form of Cecelia, her blond hair fanned youthfully across the pillow. At my back, the wind had picked up slightly and blew the smell of salt and the sound of Sanjiv's liquid voice up the island.

When I looked down to the pool that eddied between the two fist-shaped rock outcroppings, even more perfectly visible from this height, the shaded light was green at that hour. The water was clear down to the sand, the slow-moving parrot fish, and Sanjiv, who held Blaze in his arms like a baby just above the surface. Sanjiv said something just before he leaned down. I knew that he would drown Blaze then—and wasn't that right for these lovers?—and I would be spared. I wouldn't stop it. Sanjiv kissed Blaze on the mouth and I waited. The currents rocked them, but still Sanjiv wouldn't let Blaze go. I knew at that moment he couldn't do it; he was waiting for me.

By the time I made it down to the eddying pool, I had no idea how long Blaze had been in the water. His skin was a puckered grayish white, and he looked as bad as a person can look and still be alive. There would be no startling transformation when he died, just the relief of pain and the boredom of this. To end it now would be a mercy. Sanjiv placed Blaze, chilled and practically weightless, in my arms. Blaze didn't open his eyes, and there was no struggle as I lowered him and pulled away my hands. His body darkened the water below the surface and warmed it.

Later I watched the island police prepare to take Blaze's body away. Sanjiv had his arm around Cecelia, who told him she had felt a pinch behind her ear earlier, when she was in bed. She wanted to know if he thought it had occurred at the same moment Henry died. Sanjiv said yes, it seemed they were connected that way.

Tell me what happened, an island authority said to me.

What had I seen? Two men swimming in a dangerous spot, so I'd gone to help them. I told the authority, whom I'd known since childhood, that Blaze was sick and weak. Sanjiv watched me as though I understood everything now; I had offered my island, and an act of love is no crime. So I said that Henry had drowned, and he seemed to understand the power of the currents when I showed him the exact spot where it had happened.

THE COVE *by* GINA BERRIAULT

A native of Northern California, GINA BERRIAULT (1926–1999) is the author of four novels and three short story collections. In "The Cove," a realtor sells an idyllic seaside home to a young, golden family, but fails to disclose the danger haunting its shores. The story was first published in Esquire *in 1969 and later in Berriault's short story collection* Women in Their Beds, *which received the National Book Critics Circle Award and the PEN/Faulkner Award for Fiction in 1997.*

SOMETIMES THE REALTOR'S listings book will fall open to the photographs of homes not within the means of the couple on the other side of the desk, and the wife will put out her hand, almost instinctively, to see what is beyond them. Of the several properties, the couple will pause longest over a particular house on the leeward side of the island. The woman will wish aloud that they could afford it, laughing, sighing, drooping, indecorous in a time that calls for reserve, while the husband will nod and agree robustly, even goddamning. They select, after the usual excursions with the realtor to several houses within the city and on its expanding edge, a house not much different from the one back home. The property that they coveted is shown only to those fortunate families for whom every hour is opportune. Persons who sometimes roam through houses they cannot afford in order to impress the realtor, or—though they have not met him before—vindictively waste his time, never venture onto the verdant grounds and across the threshold of that property. It is much too ideal to violate with one's lack of promise or even with that vindictiveness against the realtor that asks for no reason for itself. Whoever might have in mind to dare an excursion is deterred by what might be suspicion on the part of the realtor: although everything is amiable and potential as they sit around his desk, elbows almost touching, knees almost touching, hands touching over maps and matches, a gulf suddenly divides him and them.

THE REALTOR UNLOCKED the wrought-iron gate, swung it open and stepped aside, waiting until all the members of the family had passed into the garden. Following at a discreet distance in order not to interfere with their breathtaking entry into a domain certain to be theirs and free of intruders such as himself, he bowed his head to choose the next key from the green leather case in the palm of his hand—both case and keys given him by the owner. The father went first along the path, his index finger held by the youngest of the four children, a girl of two who was walking clumsily on her toes. They were followed by the two boys, one twelve, the other nine, both lean, both wearing tan knee shorts and white pullovers edged thinly with red. The eldest, a girl of sixteen, strolled behind the boys, the wide pleats of her short white skirt parting and closing. The mother, young in spite of the number of her children, was the last of the procession except for the realtor who was, respectfully, not a part of it, following the mother by a yard, observing as if against his will how the flowers in the cloth of her dress vibrated with the movements of her body and with their own disputing colors. In the center of the emerald dusk of fern and bamboo and flowering shrubs, the father paused and so the rest paused. The garden was filled with a humming that seemed to emanate from its own exuberance until it became apparent that the sound was the sea's constant humming rising up through the density of mountain stone. Two myna birds flew up from a lichee tree in the garden, flapping over the road and settling in a breadfruit tree high on the upper slope.

The realtor unlocked the heavy teak door, found that it stuck, and pushed, his brow against it. The members of the family fanned out across the large room toward the wall of sliding glass that gave them an immense view of the sea. The realtor slid open one segment of the glass and they walked out across the terrace and over to the stone wall, and all, leaning there, gazed out on the masses of land to each side, tremendous green shoulders of earth that seemed to recede and swell in the hot light; gazed down on the vertical, winding stone stairs and, at its foot, far down, the cove. Black, volcanic rocks edged the cove, molding it into the shape of a three-quarter moon. The sea broke on the barricading reef and, after heaving and swelling on the inward side of the reef, swept almost languidly across the cove, breaking again.

The realtor took the liberty of leaning his elbows on the wall, along with the rest of them. The soft, ascending wind pressed his shirt—so white it shone in the sun—against his chest. For a few moments the shirt beat against his chest as if stirred by the beat of his heart, then the wind continued up and his shirt hung loosely again, unstirring. He was neither tall nor short, neither fat nor lean, but this averageness was like a happy medium he had attained by his own efforts. The surface of his face was receptive of all reasonable requests; under the surface, as if it were a matter of modesty, lay a look of gratification for pleasures granted to past clients. In the eyes of the father, who was a shrewd man and who considered shrewdness a virtue, the realtor was a simple man, lacking shrewdness. The realtor was silent while they gazed down, musing and exclaiming, as if even one word might be an intrusion as intolerable as an uninvited guest down with them in that pricelessly private cove.

When they began to enter back into the house to inspect the rooms, the realtor walked by the side of the father, pointing out the stoutness of beams, the solidity of the teak floors, the lavish use of marble. Servants were no problem, he told them, although he would advise them not to inquire at the village. They might find someone there, but someone unreliable who would prefer to reside in the village and come to work in the morning, if that someone felt so inclined. In his office was a list of servants with references, and one couple—Japanese—he heartily recommended. The realtor did not accompany the father and older children down to the cove. He remained in the house, strolling from room to room with the mother and the little girl, and waiting with them in the garden for the others to climb up.

The father returned carrying the coat of his dark mainland suit over his shoulder. His tie hung over the other shoulder, the land mass on which the house was perched, all seemed to comprise an initiation. They were more conscious than ever that they dwelled on an island. On more pleasant days it had begun to be as habitually under their feet as the continent they had been born to. Now the heat loosed the moorings of the island and of the memory, and the continent itself seemed to have been no more solidly in place than the island. The children swam in the morning and again in the afternoon, played cards and other games under the three large umbrellas on the sand, and indolently amused themselves in the house. The mother took her dips in the morning before anyone was up. The air was already warm and the sun bright, but a diffident presence was with her: a coolness that she was certain she would not have found had her family accompanied her. The father swam in the afternoon with the children. Each parent had a time that favored him.

After his swim, the father lay prone on the sand, his feet toward the land, his head toward the sea. He closed his eyes, hearing the water, the barking of the small black poodle running back and forth in the shallows, and the voices of the smaller children under the umbrellas. He lifted his head from his arms to face the other way, glancing out to the figures borne high on the serene, incoming swell. Three were more or less in a row, the fourth, his elder son, was at a farther distance, treading water. He laid his head down again and did not see the boy tossed into the air. One of the younger boys on the sand saw and laughed at what he thought was his cousin's amazing antic. His son's scream came to the father in two ways: it came over the water and it came through the sand, reverberating against his body. The boy was in the same spot, his arms raised. A few yards from the boy a dark fin detached itself from the dark, swarming spots that plagued the father's vision in the intense light, circled the boy, and disappeared. The boy disappeared with it, lost like the fin in the glittering air and water.

Their excitement in the water deafened the rest of the children to the terror in the cry. The father running into the water was a common sight to them, and their abiding in the water for so many more hours of the day gave them, as usual, a secret sense of their superior adaptability. The great, dark body gliding past them and around and beneath them sent them to shore as clumsily and eccentrically as if they had never learned to swim. The children under the umbrellas huddled down on their haunches, facing the sea or facing the cliffs, screaming the name of the creature. The father felt the shark pass under him and glimpsed it, and his own body seemed to dissolve, as if that languidly, monstrously gliding creature destroyed him without touching him. Way above the cove a child was climbing the steps, screaming up to the house the same word as the children below, and stumbling on the dog that ran up before him and stopped and ran up farther, barking all the way.

The daughter, with the help of the older boys, pushed the small dinghy across the sand and out into the water. Alone, to leave room in the boat for her father and brother, she rowed out to the place where her father was diving and waited there, the boat rocking and tugging away from her oars. She watched for the fin and for the large, dark body again, sighting neither within the great bowl of water, luminous, clear, except for the

111

spreading and separating patch of blood a yard from the boat. The father rose and dove again, rose and clung to the side of the boat, and the sound of his breath was the sound of their terror as they drifted, rocked by the water and by the boat's own rocking. When he had rested for a few minutes he dove again and when he rose he lifted up to her the body of the boy. Her thin arms straining, she held to the body against the tug and drag of the water while her father swung himself up into the boat. Then together they drew the body up.

THE REALTOR UNLOCKED THE GATE and stepped aside to permit the family to precede him. The family crossed the garden, the children, a small boy, and a girl, maneuvering around and between their parents in order to lead the way. Not all of the family were present. Two of the older children were in boarding school and a third child was in college. Rain had fallen only a few minutes before; steam was rising along the roof and a glittering was going on in the shade of the garden. A few doves were stirring in the trees. When the realtor moved toward the house the parents followed without lingering. The realtor spoke very little as he led the way out onto the terrace and back through the rooms, as if words were unnecessary since it was obvious that the property was to belong to this family. The mother was confused by the certainty. Before marriage she had been a hungry actress, and the years of her marriage—only the two younger children were hers—had not overcome her mistrust of certainty. She felt the need to catch the eye of the realtor and, even if her glance appeared to be flirtatious, convey to him her desire to comply. He did not meet her eyes but, his head bowed as if in solemn understanding, he moved away to lead the family farther.

alongside us, and the two guys looked over at us, and we looked at them. The guard had a shotgun. He went and spoke to the driver. Then they turned around and drove away. I had been happy there at the blackjack table, beating the slit-eyed dealer, but with the sudden heat and the run down the road, the airplane food and the funny smell of this fertile jungle, I wanted to puke.

We were staying in a bungalow beside the main building, one of a row of cottages in the trees along the beach. Diane went into the bathroom without a word. I was so freaked out that I didn't know what to do. I didn't want that cash in there with us, so after she went to sleep I walked around back, behind the cabin, and buried the money in the sand. It was dark.

Then I got into bed. I listened to Diane breathe. I couldn't tell if she was asleep or not, and I'd become afraid of that lately, of not knowing—and of how it didn't matter. We hadn't had sex since Thanksgiving. Diane said her ass was too fat. We hadn't enjoyed each other's company now in a long time, and before this trip there were nights when we didn't speak. Earlier that day, standing in line at the airport with all our luggage, she said to me, "I'm fat. I feel ugly."

I said, "We're going on a great vacation, so try to have fun."

She said, "You hate me." I didn't know what to say. I did hate her, partly, she was right, but not for being fat: Diane is small and cute, everything on her is round and full anyway. But I was taking it very seriously that she was repulsed by me, that she stopped me anytime I tried to touch her.

I still felt love for her, too, but we didn't have the same outlook anymore. And I didn't like listening to her complain all the time. My life was going the way I always thought it should—I mean my job, and money. The contracts I'd sold last quarter were huge, my company had just bought a smaller firm and merged, we were booming—and I had nobody to tell that to. Diane's job was a total disappointment, or so she claimed, though she could never be specific. She mentioned getting a master's in something, or learning to make jewelry, but that might be too complicated. At home, she ate frozen Snickers bars in bed. She made Kool-Aid every night and chugged it from the pitcher. I hadn't seen Diane in her underwear in months, or her bare shoulders or her pretty chest, or her pale, round thighs; she said she was flab, pure Jell-O; she said her potbelly hung over the waist of her skirt. At night she'd put on her big purple sweatshirt that came down to her knees; she'd pull the hood up over her head and tie the string and get into bed and turn off the lights. It got so messed up that I couldn't even kiss her—she'd laugh or cover her lips and say, "I have to wax my mustache." We had more money now, and sometimes we discussed doing something new, either kids or a new house; neither one felt like the natural thing, but what were we going to do next? Something was missing. We needed the next phase, and we needed what was missing to get to the next phase. I didn't know whether to be worried or not.

THE NEXT MORNING I went out to get the money I'd buried in the sand. As I was digging, I saw it all again in my mind, the banged-up jeep turning and then Diane running. Who knows what those guys wanted—they probably thought we were crazy—but it occurred to me then that she'd never looked back. What if I'd tripped? Maybe I missed something, but I felt terrible then, remembering: Diane, running away from me. The money was all wet; I'd packed it in a plastic bag, and a jogger who walked by wondered if it was shellfish I caught.

I had the hotel clerk change it into big bills and put it in the vault. He assured me that nothing bad had ever happened here, and never would, that I was perfectly safe. The natives were friendly, he said; I should forget it and begin to enjoy myself.

The food area was a vast tented pavilion, with plush, oversized chairs and an enormous breakfast buffet of all different kinds of exotic food. I had the cook make me an omelette. He was dark black, like the guys from the night before. I looked over at Diane, who had a couple of orange slices and a banana on her plate. I said, "Hey, come on, eat something. We're on vacation." She said that she didn't want to get too full.

As we walked to the water, I said I liked her new straw hat. She said, "If you stare at my gut I will kill you."

I rubbed some sunscreen on. The beach was totally empty. Where the hell was everybody? "Jesus Christ," I said to Diane, "this is some fucking resort."

At lunch the place was full, though, and then the crowd came to the beach, and later that afternoon there was a softball game and we joined in. I got a hit that went over the shortstop's head. Diane pitched for the other team and somehow lobbed strikes. That evening we ate pasta and shellfish. They had drummers in the pavilion, but we were too tired to stay for more than a minute, and I slept that night the way you'd hope to sleep on vacation—like a five-year-old kid with no troubles. I dreamed about my base hit and woke up to birds singing outside the window. We had pancakes for breakfast, and later the staff organized a big tug-of-war and a sack

118

race, and we met some more of the other guests. Our team won the sack race but lost the tug-of-war.

WE CLAIMED A SPOT FOR OURSELVES on the beach. Every morning you could find us there. We spent our day swimming, napping, baking in the sun. After a couple of days your eyes don't fight the landscape. The beach was gorgeous; it started at the dock and wound along for half a mile, narrow in some places, funneling into a rocky point with a jetty. The ocean was blue—deep, brilliant turquoise—except that at noon, with the sun directly overhead, it turned the color of tin. Low tide left lumps of seaweed like piles of old, wet wigs; guys came by with rakes and took them away. On the rim of the beach there were big palm trees to lie under. It was cool in the shade. If you waved to one of the staff guys, he'd bring you a chaise.

119

We got used to it. I figured out how you adjust your chaise without chopping off a finger. Where to go to eat lunch, which way to the Tiki Bar. I found a shortcut through the pricker bushes to the cottage. It's a resort, so it's yours as much as it is anybody's. You know some other people now, so you say hello. I sat there staring at the water and thought back to my life: breakfast meetings, angry clients, me in a rage at the office, somebody crying, somebody quitting, me driving back home wondering what kind of mood we'll both be in that night—days come in like the surf, and I'm sand, I'm the rocks, and it pounds me.

Diane bought a flowered bikini in the hotel store. She looked floral in it, but she wrapped a towel around her waist whenever she stood up. Her hair looked shiny in the sun. Her skin was getting darker. Then the sun would go behind a cloud, she'd tuck her hair behind her ear and turn a page, the wind would come up off the ocean—and I'd see her nipples through the fabric of her bathing suit and I'd have to look away. Her body was soft, round peaches. I'd think, Don't rush it. You'll make a fool of yourself. I wondered what the hell we were going to do.

WE WERE HAVING LUNCH ONE DAY under the big top, and this couple came up and introduced themselves. Their names were Rick and Joanie. They had just got there the night before and were staying in the bungalow right next to ours, it turned out. Our table was empty, and we invited them to sit. He was an outdoor-type guy, tall and athletic, with a mustache—he had on a black tank top, with smooth, flat muscles underneath it—and she was tall and fit with sandy blond hair, like him. They were already tan. They hadn't gotten their plates yet, so we told them what the better dishes were on the buffet and what to steer clear of, and what they run out of every day, and like that.

Rick said, "Have you tried the goatfish?" He told us the fish was a delicacy here. When they came back with food, they had some of that fish on their plates and brought an extra piece for us to try.

They lived in northern Florida. Joanie was an actress. She said she did a lot of local television commercials. She had huge teeth and a big, wide smile. When we stood up, later, I realized she was about a foot taller than me. Rick sold powerboats; he had two dealerships and a third one on the way. He had broad shoulders and big hands, a thin nose and smooth skin, and a steel diving watch on his left wrist. I'm not that tall, or as good-looking as some guys, but I'm not an ugly fucking freak or anything. These two were perfect, though. They looked like models, big models who lifted weights. They had a boy, five, and a girl, two, and they showed us pictures of them, and Rick had a picture of himself on his Harley, giving the thumbs-up. I said they must still be exhausted from the flight, but Rick pulled his hair back in a rubber band and said he'd already reserved a court for paddle tennis later.

He asked me what I thought of the fish. I said it was good. Rick said they really knew how to cook it here; it tasted like butter.

THE NEXT MORNING I was walking down the beach and I saw Rick. He said, "Hey, neighbor, where you going?"

I said, "Nowhere," and Rick said, "I'm going fishing. Come on." I'd never been fishing. I ran back to our suite. Diane was taking a nap. I didn't know what to bring. I grabbed my Swiss Army knife and left a note: "Didn't want to wake you up, honey—Rick and I went fishing."

The resort chartered a boat twice a week to take people out, and besides us there were seven or eight other guests on board. It headed toward the horizon, loud and stinking of diesel fuel. Then they shut the engine off and everybody dropped their lines. It was amazing out there. Rick fished. I didn't fish. I watched the other people.

I saw a couple of sailboats and some birds—it was quiet this far from shore—and if you stared over the side into the water you could make out the bottom, thirty or forty feet down. Rick kept taking things out of his pockets: a piece of gum, a chunk of bait, a pill from a bottle of medicine, a visor, a box of Tic-Tacs. He put on sunscreen and smoothed his mustache. Then his rod snagged—it was so bent I thought he would snap it—and he pulled a fish right out of the water, a beautiful, flat, wide fish, shimmering aquamarine color. It had incredible skin. He held it up; it was flipping around like crazy. I'd never seen a fish like that. I wasn't sure if he wanted to keep it or throw it back, but he laid it on the deck and stepped on it and stuck a knife into its head. Then he threw it in a Ziploc bag.

"That right there," he said, "is good eating." I watched as the interior of the bag fogged over with moisture. I think the fish was still moving.

I said, "Is it dead?"

He said, "What do you mean?"

"Would you kill it, please?"

He said, "It's dead."

"Is that goatfish?"

"That? No."

WE HAD BEERS FROM A COOLER and watched the other people fish. There was a woman across from us wearing a thing like a black slip and drinking a Coke. Rick said, "Look at her. She's incredible. My dick's been hard the whole day."

She looked like *Breakfast at Tiffany's*—that actress with the skinny neck. I smiled at her. She smiled back. "Guess what," Rick said. "She wants to fuck you." They started the engine again, and we cruised along the water, spray coming over the side and hitting us. He kept staring at the woman. She flipped her long black hair, talking with the captain, and turned her beautiful ass in our direction. She was small and had a girl's waist and tan shoulders. Her legs were perfect. He said, "What I'd do to get my rocket off in her." The boat was turning around then. We headed back.

They let us out at the dock, a short way from the buildings and the people lying out on the sand. We came walking up the beach with Rick's fish, and Rick went someplace to clean it. The women, Joanie and Diane, were lying side by side.

"Look at this," Diane said, and sat up to show me the back of her head. "Joanie did this to my hair." It was all braided in teeny rows. She was excited.

"That's wild, honey," I said. "Thanks, Joanie."

She said, "No problem." She was propped up on her elbow, with her free hand covering her eyes like a visor. She squinted into the sun, smiling hopefully.

"Here," I said, and tossed her my baseball hat.

"Thanks," she said, and pulled it down and swung her ponytail out the back. I looked at Diane—her mouth was hanging open in surprise. Did she want my hat for herself? I guess so.

She slid down to wipe the sand off her feet, and I knelt beside her and kissed her. I took her hand and held it. I ducked down and kissed her neck. She giggled and said to Joanie, "Maybe I should get my ears pierced." Joanie was staring down the beach looking for her husband. She was already very tan and had a swimmer's body—taut, trim, and lanky; she had beautiful bosoms, and her hipbones jutted up so nicely you could've hung Christmas ornaments on them. I kissed Diane's throat and held her thin braids in my hand. She jerked her head way. "My hair's filthy," she said. Joanie looked down the blanket at us, over the delicate arch of her pelvis, and smiled.

THE FOUR OF US SAT TOGETHER at dinner that night and drank wine. I ate this fish stew in a flaky pie crust, and after dinner the staff built a bonfire on the beach and we took another bottle of wine and went down there.

They'd dragged big logs over for us to sit on, and I sat down next to the guy stoking the fire. It was chilly out. The fire was heating up one side of my face, making it swell, and the sea breeze hit me on the other side and it felt numb. The local guys were talking to each other a mile a minute—it was totally unintelligible—and across the circle I saw Diane chatting with a couple we'd met on the airport van.

Our vacation was half over. On the whole, things were better. Was that what Diane thought, too? Or had she stopped loving me, and couldn't say so? I kept wondering if this was the end. I was sitting in a jolly crowd of people. I sipped my wine. Rick was standing over on the side, talking with the woman from the boat; he opened her beer for her with a thing on his key chain and took a swig. The girl laughed. Joanie was two feet away from them. She still had that dopey smile plastered on her face. She sat Indian style on the sand, looking tan and tired, watching the fire.

After a minute, Rick sat down. He was wearing white tennis shorts and a flannel shirt with the sleeves ripped off, and I thought, What kind of guy brings a ripped shirt with him on vacation? It was cold out, and everybody else was wearing jackets. He didn't seem cold. The fire glowed in his golden hair. He had dimples next to his mouth, and he wore his hair long and curly. He moved down the log right next to me. He was tan as hell, his arm muscles were like knotted brown wood. Rick had the looks—handsome and strong and cool at the same time, that was him. Like those guys you knew in high school who had it all. He probably used to drive a Camaro with a surfboard on it.

On the other side of the circle there were two hotel guys playing guitars. They weren't spectacular or terrible, but one guy had a nice voice. Rick asked me how everything was; we talked about home, how it seemed like a million miles away. I started to tell him about my problems, my crummy sex life with Diane. I don't know why—people do funny things on vacation.

He listened, staring into the fire. I tried to keep the descriptions as vague as possible, and then I thought, fuck it—some stupid boat dealer from the Everglades who I'm never gonna see again, so what if he knows my wife has a mustache? He said he understood. He was, it turned out, totally cool. We talked about how married people get along together. He rubbed his chin. "That's all normal," he said. "You have to work around it."

So, as Diane and I walked back to our suite, I grabbed some matches and asked for a candle from the front desk. Following Rick's advice, I gave Diane a neck rub, and put some warm water in a bowl and got a washcloth. I washed her neck and shoulders with the cloth. She asked me what I was doing, and I told her to be quiet. I washed her hands and her fingers; I untied her sandals and washed the tops of her feet. She said, "That feels good." I put some lotion on her elbows. She let me undress her. I took her shirt off, and her bra; I undid her shorts and pulled them off. She lay down and smiled, and I took the cloth and rubbed it in slow circles over her entire body.

I loved her, I still knew that. This was my princess here. We weren't going to die from this. I sat beside her, and we talked about the trip so far, the dinners, the bonfire, those guys in the jeep who were trying to kill us. She'd signed up for a windsurfing lesson for later in the week and was all excited about going. I put some moisturizer on her shoulders and brushed her hair, and then I took all my clothes off and lay there next to her. We seemed happy. She was cute as hell. In the past four days, the sun had made her hair lighter. Her arms and legs were dark, and her tummy was a lighter shade of tan; where the bikini had been was pure white. I mentioned a few things about life at home, how we needed to make some changes, to plan for the future. Diane had her arm under her head, and every few minutes she shut her eyes. Her eyelids were almost white against her tan face. When I asked her if she was sleepy she said no. We stayed like that for a while.

It reminded me of a scene out of high school—the candle on the table, both of us buzzed on wine, my dick wanging around between us. I looked down the length of her body and put my hand on her. She didn't move. I was thinking the way I had in high school, too—like I would do anything just to touch her. She yawned. I pictured doing it to her even if she passed out. Diane said, "Excuse me." I was dying to fuck my wife. I was sizzling. As soon as I tried something—I moved myself against her and put my lips on her neck—she jumped back and a look crossed her face; she said my beard was scratchy. And then she started talking a mile a minute about the woman in the cabin next to Joanie's who'd seen an iguana, how it ran across her foot and disappeared into the woods, and we lay there, nobody saying a word now. In a few more minutes, I heard her breathing change. The candle was still going, flickering alongside us. She'd fallen asleep.

THE NEXT DAY, as we were eating our jambalaya for lunch, they came by. Joanie asked Diane if she wanted to go shopping. Diane said yes, and Rick said he'd rented a mountain bike and heard of some trails that went up into the hills, if I was interested. I didn't feel like it, and with everybody gone I went into our room and called my office. I turned on my computer and faxed them some stuff, and spent an hour on the phone with our comptroller—we'd had a scare with a big supplier, but it was O.K. now. I returned some other calls. Everything was fine. At four o'clock I looked up. The day was ending. There were three days left of our vacation, it had flown by, and what the fuck was I doing crapping around inside?

I walked toward the hotel's plaza, feeling pale and tired. My hands were sweaty. I hated myself for missing the sun and now the ocean was calm and the breeze had died. Salt covered everything— 127 stones, leaves, the spotlights sticking up every five feet in the ground. I walked back and forth between the tennis courts and the place where we usually sat on the beach. There were some European-looking dudes in our spot, wearing skimpy Speedos; I felt like walking up to them and kicking in their skulls. I didn't see anyone I knew, as if a whole crew of fresh guests, all ghostly white and uncomfortable, had come in the night before and replaced the old ones. A woman stood next to me with her baby, changing its diaper in the middle of the plaza, stinking up the joint with her kid's smelly dump. When I finally saw a familiar face go by—the kitchen-staff guy who made my omelettes—I was so relieved I almost hugged him. He was carrying a three-foot-long fish—a tuna, he said, seventy pounds; it had just come off a boat. I followed him to an outdoor kitchen, and while he cut it up I asked him about growing up on the island.

Later I was sitting in the lobby, reading the newspaper, when Rick came in with his bicycle. He had on tight black bicycle-rider pants, and his thick, muscular legs were all tan and defined, with big veins on his calves. He said the ride had been "killer," and showed me on a map where he'd gone. Then he pulled me up by the arm with his iron grip and yanked off his sunglasses—he had a raccoon stripe of white where the glasses had been. Talking low, he told me there were guys out there living forty feet up in the trees, pot growers with machines guns who almost shot him but then took him in and befriended him. He said they were the most amiable guys, and he talked with them and smoked pot and sang reggae. They gave him a tour of their jungle hideout. They'd made crude musical instruments out of tin boxes and wire, and they had their feet propped up on crates of ammo. He said, "One of them went to Oxford."

I said, "Congratulations."

He said, "They ship the pot out in these carved heads, the dark wood carving this area is known for, called *obiko*. Joanie was supposed to buy one when she went into town today. They stuff the shit into a hollowed-out part of the heads and ship them around the world."

I said, "Is that so?"

Rick said, "Listen, come back up with me tomorrow. You can't believe the view."

I said, "Not in a million years."

"I'm taking Joanie," he said.

"You're not taking Joanie up there. They'll gang-rape her."

"They're the friendliest people in the world. They gave me

dope. They had piles of it laying around." He started to reach into his bicycle pants, in the middle of the lobby. He said, "I got it here somewhere."

"Rick—what the fuck are you doing?" I said, and grabbed his hand.

He said, "Possession of marijuana is not a crime here. And even if it is, they want the tourists to smoke it."

DIANE ASKED RICK TO TELL THE WHOLE STORY again at dinner. I was sick of it and said nothing. I was going gambling again at that little shack. It was "casino night," whatever that meant. Rick went with me. I agreed on the condition that he leave his wacky weed at home. Diane stayed with Joanie. There was a lounge singer in the nightclub, and they went to see his act.

129

The casino was busier that night. There were lines for the slot machines and a crowd at every table. I played blackjack. I ate about a thousand pounds of salty cashews and didn't drink. Rick stood next to me, and after an hour a seat opened up at the table and he decided to play.

"I'll be your wingman," he said, stacking his chips in ten-dollar piles.

Blackjack is pretty simple: You need some luck, you need to be able to add up to twenty-one, and like that. I've seen all kinds of systems, basic card counting, charts guys carry with statistical analysis; I've seen guys with backers—professionals—and I've seen people asked to leave casinos for various offenses. Rick bet erratically, in no particular pattern; I couldn't tell if he had any experience at all, and I watched him rip through his bank and go back to the cashier for more chips. He talked to himself and filled up on vodka, and when his bank was gone he went back another time. I couldn't bear to look. He bummed a cigarette off somebody and mentioned going water-skiing in the morning, and told me how he gave up smoking, cold turkey, on New Year's Day. "This is my first puff in a month," he said.

I said, "If you get rid of that hand, you might not lose as fast." He ignored me.

Meanwhile, I did well. I'm good at math, and blackjack is a lot of math. At one point, the dealer aimed his finger at me and said, "You're tough," and I shrugged. I felt like David Hasselhoff. I pointed back at him and then didn't say a word except when I needed a card. Rick was out, he'd played like an imbecile, and he stayed to watch me, hunched over in his skintight rugby shit.

130   I took a card. The dealer busted. I watched all the hopeful people around me losing money, and then a new dealer took over, and I cashed in almost nine hundred bucks. I won, and the house lost. As we walked back to the hotel—it wasn't even midnight, and it was cool and breezy like every other night since I'd arrived—Rick asked me to give him his money back. It was five hundred dollars. He said, "Please, buddy." I tried to tell him that the money he lost was no longer his money—it was the bank's—and what I had was different money, not his. He started explaining: He said he'd been drunk, the rules were different here from the ones in the casino he played in, whatever. I said to him, "Why don't you go for a swim?" He said no. He begged me. I started laughing and pretended to play the violin. He told me Joanie had refused to let him take the money for gambling, but he'd taken it anyway, and now he'd blown it, and he needed the money before we got back or she'd kill him. I said no.

He asked me one more time. "What do I look like?" I said. "Get an advance on your credit card."

We got to Rick and Joanie's cabin. I could hear the women inside. I said to him, "Next time you gamble you need to have a figure in your head, a top amount you can lose," but he told me to shut up. Then he opened the door, and we went inside.

The women said the lounge singer was a Caribbean man named Mr. High-Five, and started dancing around the bed. Diane had ordered two pizzas from room service and there was food all over the place. Rick sat in a chair in the corner with his hat on backward. He looked fried, as if he got a sunburn on the bike that day. Diane and I went to our room.

We were in bed with the lights off when Rick knocked at the door. I went outside and stood on the paved path with him. The moon was shining on the water. He'd been crying. I could see where the discussion was about to go. He wore wrinkled blue boxers and white socks. He'd taken his hat off, and I noticed he had hives on his forehead, probably from riding his bike through the jungle.

He said he felt like crap inside. He said he loved me, he told me he was so surprised to find a friend at one of these places that he couldn't believe his luck. "You know what I mean?" he said. I saw the light was on in their room, which meant Joanie probably knew he'd lost the money. He was talking about the fish we'd caught together. "There's nothing like fishing with your friend," he said. His oratory didn't seem to be rounding any corners. There were so many different stupid things about this moment, now he was telling me he got ripped off buying some Krugerrands, I wanted him to shut the fuck up, I didn't know what to do, I went back into my bungalow and got five hundred dollars from the night's winnings and handed it to him. I said, "Here."

He said, "Thank you."

I didn't answer him. I thought he was full of shit.

He went back in and shut the door. I stood there, outside my door, furious at myself. His light went off. I distinctly heard him say something to Joanie. I waited another minute. I didn't hear anything else.

My watch said 2 A.M. A mosquito came up and bit my eyelid, but I didn't feel like going inside yet. I was sweating. Right next door, if I needed them, were my new friend Rick and his piece-of-ass wife. And in my bungalow I had my own no-fuck, don't-touch wife sleeping off her pizza pies. I had a view of the ocean, the seaborne air, mountains in back of me, jungles full of tree-climbing pot freaks. In the moonlight, there were swans or storks, maybe pelicans, gliding above the calm sea, looking for a fish to spear.

THE NEXT DAY'S WEATHER was like all the others. Diane and I swam and read our books and lay on the beach. Joanie appeared at lunch and joined us; she looked tired, and the three of us said almost nothing as we ate. I asked about Rick, and she shrugged, and from then on we baked in the sun, watching the water. Joanie told us she'd talked to her kids that morning; their grandpa had made them spaghetti sandwiches, and they loved it. We swam, and later Joanie said Rick was probably playing tennis, and at dinner, when we still didn't see him, she said he was exhausted and had never woken up from his nap.

We said goodnight and went to bed. This time it was Diane

who started up. She kissed me and I kissed her back. I held her tits. She opened my shorts and massaged me with a feathery touch of her fingertips, kind of teasing.

It went on for, I don't know, a while. There was all this circling, circling—had she forgotten how to do everything? She was doing a terrible job. I couldn't stand it anymore, I shoved her out of the way and started rubbing myself. It was not a scene I'd recommend—not loving, if you know what I mean, not the expression of the subtle union between two people. And then Diane started to cry. She said she felt like a failure in every way—I was ready to agree—and then she went the other way and said I didn't know her anymore, that I'd forgotten how it used to be when we were crazy about each other, that now I didn't give a fuck about anything but making money. She cried and I held her. I regretted whacking off like that, I admitted it made everything worse. But I didn't really care. Without any more fighting, we both fell asleep.

FIRST THING FRIDAY MORNING, Diane went off to that windsurfing lesson in the bay. Joanie and I sat on the beach and talked. There was still no sign of Rick.

I told her about my business. She said it sounded fascinating. She told me there was a soap opera based in Miami that she was thinking about trying out for. We went swimming. I blew bubbles out my nose, and it cracked her up. Breakfast ended at eleven, and neither of us did anything about it. Eventually I got up and bought us apples at the commissary.

Rick showed up around noon, all sweaty in a tennis outfit and a purple baseball hat with the name of the resort stitched across it.

I'd actually missed having him around. Rick's eyes were so green they almost glowed, from all that time in the sun. He was grinning again. Joanie asked if he was hungry; he said no. He had a white plastic bucket and a fishing rod; he went over near the dock and began surf casting.

Joanie was looking at me. I didn't know what she meant. I said, "What are you smiling for?"

She said, "I'm such a fucking idiot."

Diane came back. She was all excited. She sat in the sand and told us how she got the Windsurfer going—it was tricky—and how the instructor, Phillipe, and she and two others went way out into the ocean. She said she'd never had so much fun in her life. The group had had to turn back because the weather was starting to change, but not before they spotted a giant sea turtle, swimming alongside them. She said, "It was huge and gray—it had slimy bumps on its back." I just looked off to the horizon, but I couldn't see anything, just a few clouds in a long line above the water.

Diane jumped up to go say hello to Rick over by the dock. They started chatting, and soon she was holding the rod and Rick was leaning around her, showing her how to draw it back with his long, bronze muscles. Rick was tall and broad-shouldered, and Diane was looking up at him. You could hear them laugh. Joanie sat beside me, blinking into the hazy sun, her lips coated in a thick film of sunblock. After a few minutes I laid my head down, and when I looked up Diane and Rick were gone. I took my shirt off and fell asleep.

I woke up to the wind kicking up the sand, just the way Phillipe had said. My mouth was dry. The sun was gone.

The beach was empty. I sat up, my face mashed into wrinkles

from the towel. Joanie had passed out, too, curled up beside me in her bikini bottoms and my gray T-shirt. I sat back and looked at her small pink feet, the calluses on her heels and toes, her smooth, hairless thighs, the faint hint of veins beneath the skin. The stretched back of her red bikini bottoms across her dynamite ass. It was so pretty I wanted to cry. She yawned, reaching her long, thin arms up, and I saw her bikini top lying next to her on the towel.

Joanie sat up on her knees, beside me. "Where did they go?" she said. I didn't know. She'd knotted my shirt so it rode high up on her rib cage. I reached across and pulled the knot. She watched me. My hand slipped underneath the T-shirt, and I felt my palm across her stomach. There was sand stuck on her leg, and I watched her braless boobs moving against the inside of my shirt. I saw her swallow. I felt her breathe.

Diane came walking up the beach from the direction of the jetty. She said she was tired, and did I want to come take a nap with her. A second later we were walking down the beach to our room. Joanie didn't have time to respond.

Diane closed the blinds. I sat down and untied my sneakers. She stepped between my legs and put her tongue against my teeth. She knelt and yanked off my bathing suit and flung it on the lampshade. I was so excited I started to shake. I sat back on the bed, flustered. She took off her bottoms, standing in front of me, and kissed my throat. I kept looking for marks on her from Rick—a sign of use on my wife's body—but I was so turned on after all this time that I was seeing spots. The place where her bikini had been was glowing. She held my head. I rubbed my face against her stomach.

We lay down and started to do it. She seemed fine, I guess. She

135

was digging it. It was the same old Diane. I held her sweet face. She said, "It's nice to see you smile again." Finally, we were grooving.

When it was over, I went into the bathroom and got a glass of water. My groin was raw. She lay on her stomach, breathing.

I sat beside her and rubbed my hand across the top of her ass, as fine as silk.

She said, "I can't move."

"So don't."

"You're the best lover in the world," she said, and turned over and held me. "I promised Rick I'd go fishing on that boat you guys went on." She looked at me. "Is it all right if I try it? It's our last day."

I said, "Absolutely." She squeezed my body. I hugged her back, as hard as she was hugging me.

"You feel so good," she said, and I said, "Um-hmm." The next second she was standing on one leg, trying to get into her panties. She said, "Thank you."

"For what?"

"For being so wonderful to me."

"No problem," I said. She ran around the room, looking for clothes. She took my baseball hat and fitted it on her head. I was still in bed. She leaned down next to me.

"You're the kind of husband women wish for." She gave me a kiss, pulling my lips with her teeth.

"O.K.," I said. She took the camera and flew out the door.

IT WAS FOUR O'CLOCK. I was on my own. I thought of going back to find Joanie on the beach. I flipped open my briefcase and then shut it, and got up and showered and left the bungalow.

I stopped by the Tiki Bar for a last drink. Jimmy, the bartender, was there, washing the bar off with a hose. The woman from the boat came, and we said hello. I hadn't seen her since the bonfire that night.

She was wearing a bikini and had a slim leather belly bag clipped around her waist. She wiggled her ass onto the next bar stool and lit a smoke and said, "Jim, what do I want?" He shoveled ice into the sink, waiting for her to answer. She said, "Rum-and-Coke, my favorite."

"I'm going back to Baltimore on Sunday. I miss my cats," she told me. She'd been here at least a week. She said, "They bill this place as a singles' resort, but I didn't see any singles here. Just me. And a couple of Swedish guys in G-strings."

I said, "How many cats?"

"Two. They're probably dead by now. My sister's been feeding them."

I was thinking about Diane. The perfume smell of her hair, the velvet softness of her baby skin. We got so close. She was floating all around me.

"I bet they're O.K.," I said. "Don't be depressed."

"I'm sick of this Tiki Bar," the woman said. I thought about Diane and Rick—what was she doing? I pictured them fishing and talking and doing whatever else you do on a boat. Diane and I were in some new place together, and I thought of how it had to keep being new, or else we were doomed. More people came. Here I was, sitting around, depressed. That's because you are a loser, I said to myself. I sipped my daiquiri. It tasted like ice cream. The woman from Baltimore was staring at me. She tapped her cigarette, waiting for me to say something else. I had nothing to say. I stared out at the water as the time passed in long sips. Out beyond the beach, I saw the cruiser pulling back into the harbor.

I said, "Hey—you like lawyers?" She asked why. "My cousin Walt is a lawyer. He's good-looking. He lives in Baltimore."

She said, "Really?"

"He has his own firm. He's loaded."

"Wow."

Walt had a lisp. He talked like Popeye. But he also had muscles and owned a house on two acres in the suburbs.

"Walt's a great guy," I said. "He'd love you." She smiled and put out her cigarette. "I'll call him when we get back."

She gave me a business card from her belly bag. "Something to look forward to," she said.

Diane and Rick came back. They'd seen dolphins, they said. Diane looked beautiful. I wanted to hold her and touch her again. Rick had caught three fish. He was carrying them in a cooler filled with ice. The long one he called a "dagger fish." He didn't know its real name. His jaw was cocked in a big smile. I stared at his straw-colored curls.

Diane sure seemed happy now. What had happened? I didn't have a clue. I thought of all the different combinations. I didn't panic—why the fuck should you panic? While I'm thinking this, though, Rick winked at the barstool next to me, at the woman, and she smiled and blushed. Diane looked at me and I looked at her and Rick. I still haven't figured out what was going on. He showed me the other two fish; he wanted to take them home in dry ice and smoke them, and send them to me in the mail. I said, "I do not accept dead fish in the mail,'' and finished my drink. Diane came over and grabbed me. I put my arm around her and held her tight. The cook ended up broiling the fish for dinner. Rick bought the wine.

"Here's to us," he said, "and fuck the mortgage." He was all smiles, and our happiness continued. Later in the evening, I found out they were a lot more than five hundred dollars behind; they had debts at home, too. It was painful. Probably all he needed to avert disaster was some sane advice, a speck of financial insight. I could give him that. I told him to call me before he made any god-awful decisions.

We drank and ate till midnight and went swimming naked while the ladies crawled around looking for shells by the light of the moon. The next morning, we rode with them to the airport, through that beautiful countryside. I was looking at everything, and it was so nice, 139 because we were leaving.

THE HANDSOMEST DROWNED MAN IN THE WORLD
by GABRIEL GARCÍA MÁRQUEZ

*Born in Colombia in 1928, GABRIEL GARCÍA
MÁRQUEZ has won the Nobel Prize in Literature, and
his work has been published in dozens of languages. In this
fantastical tale, which first appeared in* Playboy *in 1968,
the inhabitants of a tiny South American fishing village
attempt to unravel the mystery of a stranger's death, and in
doing so come to imagine a better life for themselves.*

THE FIRST CHILDREN who saw the dark and slinky bulge approaching through the sea let themselves think it was an enemy ship. Then they saw it had no flags or masts and they thought it was a whale. But when it washed up on the beach, they removed the clumps of seaweed, the jellyfish tentacles, and the remains of fish and flotsam, and only then did they see that it was a drowned man.

They had been playing with him all afternoon, burying him in the sand and digging him up again, when someone chanced to see them and spread the alarm in the village. The men who carried him to the nearest house noticed that he weighed more than any dead man they had ever known, almost as much as a horse, and they said to each other that maybe he'd been floating too long and the water had got into his bones. When they laid him on the floor they said he'd been taller than all other men because there was barely enough room for him in the house, but they thought that maybe the ability to keep on growing after death was part of the nature of certain drowned men. He had the smell of the sea about him and only his shape gave one to suppose that it was the corpse of a human being, because the skin was covered with a crust of mud and scales.

They did not even have to clean off his face to know that the dead man was a stranger. The village was made up of only twenty-odd wooden houses that had stone courtyards with no flowers and which were spread about on the end of a desert-like cape. There was so little land that mothers always went about with the fear that the wind would carry off their children and the few dead that the years had caused among them had to be thrown off the cliffs. But the sea was calm and bountiful and all the men fitted into seven boats. So when they found the drowned man they simply had to look at one another to see that they were all there.

That night they did not go out to work at sea. While the men went to find out if anyone was missing in neighbouring villages, the women stayed behind to care for the drowned man. They took the mud off with grass swabs, they removed the underwater stones entangled in his hair, and they scraped the crust off with tools used for scaling fish. As they were doing that they noticed that the vegetation on him came from faraway oceans and deep water and that his clothes were in tatters, as if he had sailed through labyrinths of coral. They noticed too that he bore his death with pride, for he did not have the lonely look of other drowned men who came out of the sea or that haggard, needy look of men who drowned in rivers. But only when they finished cleaning him off did they become aware of the kind of man he was and it left them breathless. Not only was he the tallest, strongest, most virile, and best built man they had ever seen, but even though they were looking at him there was no room for him in their imagination.

They could not find a bed in the village large enough to lay him on nor was there a table solid enough to use for his wake. The tallest men's holiday pants would not fit him, nor the fattest ones' Sunday shirts, nor the shoes of the one with the biggest feet. Fascinated by his huge size and his beauty, the women then decided to make him some pants from a large piece of sail and a shirt from some bridal brabant linen so that he could continue through his death with dignity. As they sewed, sitting in a circle and gazing at the corpse between stitches, it seemed to them that the wind had never been so steady nor the sea so restless as on that night and they supposed that the change had something to do with the dead man. They thought that if that magnificent man had lived in the village, his house would have had the widest doors, the highest ceiling, and the strongest floor, his bedstead would have been made from a midship frame held together by iron bolts, and his wife would have been the happiest woman. They thought that he would have had so much authority that he could have drawn fish out of the sea simply by calling their names and that he would have put so much work into his land that springs would have burst forth from among the rocks so that he would have been able to plant flowers on the cliffs. They secretly compared him to their own men, thinking that for all their lives theirs were incapable of doing what he could do in one night, and they ended up dismissing them deep in their hearts as the weakest, meanest, and most useless creatures on earth. They were wandering through that maze of fantasy when the oldest woman, who as the oldest had looked upon the drowned man with more compassion than passion, sighed:

"He has the face of someone called Esteban."

It was true. Most of them had only to take another look at him to see that he could not have any other name. The more stubborn among them, who were the youngest, still lived for a few hours with the illusion that when they put his clothes on and he lay among the flowers in patent leather shoes his name might be Lautaro. But it was a vain illusion. There had not been enough canvas, the poorly cut and worse sewn pants were too tight, and the hidden strength of his heart popped the buttons on his shirt. After midnight the whistling of the wind died down and the sea fell into its Wednesday drowsiness. The silence put an end to any last doubts: he was Esteban. The women who had dressed him, who had combed his hair, had cut his nails and shaved him were unable to hold back a shudder of pity when they had to resign themselves to his being dragged along the ground.

and forth, stumbling, while they released in sighs what they did not in tears, so that the men finally exploded with *since when has there ever been such a fuss over a drifting corpse, a drowned nobody, a piece of cold Wednesday meat.* One of the women, mortified by so much lack of care, then removed the handkerchief from the dead man's face and the men were left breathless too.

He was Esteban. It was not necessary to repeat it for them to recognize him. If they had been told Sir Walter Raleigh, even they might have been impressed with his gringo accent, the macaw on his shoulder, his cannibal-killing blunderbuss, but there could be only one Esteban in the world and there he was, stretched out like a sperm whale, shoeless, wearing the pants of an undersized child, and with those stony nails that had to be cut with a knife. They only had to take the handkerchief off his face to see that he was ashamed, that it was not his fault that he was so big or so heavy or so handsome, and if he had known that this was going to happen, he would have looked for a more discreet place to drown in, seriously, I even would have tied the anchor off a galleon around my neck and staggered off a cliff like someone who doesn't like things in order not to be upsetting people now with this Wednesday dead body, as you people say, in order not to be bothering anyone with this filthy piece of cold meat that doesn't have anything to do with me. There was so much truth in his manner that even the most mistrustful men, the ones who felt the bitterness of endless nights at sea fearing that their women would tire of dreaming about them and begin to dream of drowned men, even they and others who were harder still shuddered in the marrow of their bones at Esteban's sincerity.

That was how they came to hold the most splendid funeral they could conceive of for an abandoned drowned man. Some women who had gone to get flowers in the neigbouring villages returned with other women who could not believe what they had been told, and those women went back for more flowers when they saw the dead man, and they brought more and more until there were so many flowers and so many people that it was hard to walk about. At the final moment it pained them to return him to the waters as an orphan and they chose a father and mother from among the best people, and aunts and uncles and cousins, so that through him all the inhabitant of the village became kinsmen. Some sailors who heard the weeping from a distance went off course and people heard of one who had himself tied to the mainmast, remembering ancient fables about sirens. While they fought for the privilege of carrying him on their shoulders along the steep escarpment of the cliffs, men and women became aware for the first time of the desolation of their streets, the dryness of their courtyards, the narrowness of their dreams as they faced the splendour and beauty of their drowned man. They let him go without an anchor so that he could come back if he wished and whenever he wished, and they all held their breath for the fraction of centuries the body took to fall

With his mainsail beginning to luff, he had steered the big ketch a little farther off the wind, gliding toward the trail of living light in the tug's wake. Only in the last second did the dime drop; he took a quick look over his shoulder. And of course there came the barge against the moon-traced mountains, a big black homicidal juggernaut, unmarked and utterly unlighted, bearing down on them. Blessington swore and spun the wheel like Ezekiel, as hard to port as it went, thinking that if his keel was over the cable nothing would save them, that 360 degrees of helm or horizon would be less than enough to escape by.

Then everything not secured came crashing down on everything else, the tables and chairs on the afterdeck went over, plates and bottles smashed, whatever was breakable immediately broke. The boat, the *Sans Regret*, fell off the wind like a comedian and flapped into a flying jibe. A couple of yards to starboard the big barge raced past like a silent freight train, betrayed only by the slap of its hull against the waves. It might have been no more than the wind, for all you could hear of it. When it was safely gone, the day's fear welled up again and gagged him.

The Frenchman ran out on deck cursing and looked to the cockpit, where Blessington had the helm. His hair was cut close to his skull. He showed his teeth in the mast light. He was brushing his shorts; something had spilled in his lap.

"*Qu'est-ce que c'est là?*" he demanded of Blessington. Blessington pointed into the darkness where the barge had disappeared. The Frenchman knew only enough of the ocean to fear the people on it. "*Quel cul!*" he said savagely. "Who is it?" He was afraid of the Coast Guard and of pirates.

150

"We just missed being sunk by a barge. No lights. Submerged cable. It's okay now."

"Fuck," said the Frenchman, Freycinet. "Why are you stopping?"

"Stopping?" It took a moment to realize that Freycinet was under the impression that because the boat had lost its forward motion they were stopping, as though he had applied a brake. Freycinet had been around boats long enough to know better. He must be out of his mind, Blessington thought.

"I'm not stopping, Honoré. We're all right."

"I bust my fucking ass below," said Freycinet. "Marie fall out of bed."

Tough shit, thought Blessington. Be thankful you're not treading water in the splinters of your stupidly named boat. "Sorry, man," he said. 151

Sans Regret, with its fatal echoes of Piaf. The Americans might be culturally deprived, Blessington thought, but surely every cutter in the Yankee Coast Guard would have the sense to board that one. And the cabin stank of the resiny ganja they had stashed, along with the blow, under the cabin sole. No amount of roach spray or air freshener could cut it. The space would probably smell of dope forever.

Freycinet went below without further complaint, missing in his ignorance the opportunity to abuse Blessington at length. It had been Blessington's fault they had not seen the barge sooner, stoned and drunk as he was. He should have looked for it as soon as the tug went by. To stay awake through the night he had taken crystal and his peripheral vision was flashing him little mongoose darts, shooting imagined, was one of those Texans, a tough, loud man who cursed the Mexicans. She was extremely tall and rather thin, with very long legs. Her slenderness and height and interesting face had taken her into modeling, to Paris and Milan. In contrast, she had muscular thighs and a big derriere, which, if it distressed the couturiers, made her more desirable. She was Blessington's designated girlfriend on the trip but they rarely made love because, influenced by the others, he had taken an early dislike to her. He supposed she knew it.

"Oh, wow," she said in her Texas voice, "look at those pretty mountains."

It was exactly the kind of American comment that made the others all despise and imitate her—even Marie, who had no English at all. Gillian had come on deck stark naked, and each of them, the Occitan Freycinet, Norman Marie, and Irish Blessington, felt scornful and slightly offended. Anyone else might have been forgiven. They had decided she was a type and she could do no right.

Back on Canouan, Gillian had conceived a lust for one of the dealers. At first, when everyone smoked in the safe house, they had paid no attention to the women. The deal was repeated to everyone's satisfaction. As the dealers gave forth their odor of menace Marie had skillfully disappeared herself in plain view. But Gillian, to Blessington's humiliation and alarm, had put out a ray and one of the men had called her on it.

Madness. In a situation so volatile, so bloody *fraught*. But she was full of lusts, was Texan Gillian, and physically courageous, too. He noticed she whined less than the others, in spite of her irritating accent. It had ended with her following the big St. Vincentian to her guesthouse room, walking ten paces behind with her eyes down, making herself a prisoner, a lamb for the slaughter.

For a while Blessington had thought she would have to do all three of them but it had been only the one, Nigel. Nigel had returned her to Blessington in a grim little ceremony, holding her with the chain of her shark's-tooth necklace twisted tight around her neck.

"Wan' have she back, mon?"

Leaving Blessington with the problem of how to react. The big bastard was fucking welcome to her, but of course it would have been tactless to say so. Should he protest and get everyone killed? Or should he be complacent and be thought a pussy and possibly achieve the same result? It was hard to find a middle ground but Blessington found one, a tacit, ironic posture, fashioned of silences and body language. The Irish had been a subject race, too, after all.

"I gon' to make you a present, mon. Give you little pink piggy back. Goodness of my ha'art." 155

So saying, Nigel had put his huge busted-knuckle hand against her pale hard face and she had looked down submissively, trembling a little, knowing not to smile. Afterward, she was very cool about it. Nigel had given her a Rasta bracelet, beads in the red, yellow, and green colors of Ras Tafari.

"Think I'm a pink piggy, Liam?"

He had not been remotely amused and he had told her so.

So she had walked on ahead laughing and put her palms together and looked up to the sky and said, "Oh, my Lord!" And then glanced at him and wiped the smile off her face. Plainly she'd enjoyed it, all of it. She wore the bracelet constantly.

Now she leaned on her elbows against the chart table with her bare bum thrust out, turning the bracelet with the long, bony fingers into the sun. The Pitons, no closer, seemed to displease him now. "She's a bitch, *non?*"

"I think she's all right," Blessington said. "I really do."

And for the most part he did. In any case he had decided to, because an eruption of hardcore, coke-and-speed-headed paranoia could destroy them all. It had done so to many others. Missing boats sometimes turned up on the mangrove shore of some remote island, the hulls blistered with bullet holes, cabins attended by unimaginable swarms of flies. Inside, *tableaux morts* not to be forgotten by the unlucky discoverer. Strong-stomached photographers recorded the *tableaux* for the DEA's files, where they were stamped NOT TO BE DESTROYED, HISTORIC INTEREST. The agency took a certain satisfaction. Blessington knew all this from his sister and her husband in Providence.

158   Now they were almost back to Martinique and Blessington wanted intensely not to die at sea. In the worst of times, he grew frightened to the point of utter despair. It had been, he realized at such times, a terrible mistake. He gave up on the money. He would settle for just living, for living even in prison in France or America. Or at least for not dying on that horrible bright blue ocean, aboard the *Sans Regret.*

"Yeah," he told Freycinet. "Hell, I wouldn't worry about her. Just a bimbo."

All morning they tacked for the Pitons. Around noon, a great crown of puffy cloud settled around Gros Piton and they were close enough to distinguish the two peaks one from the other. Freycinet refused to go below. His presence was so unpleasant that Blessington felt like weeping, knocking him unconscious, throwing him overboard or jumping over himself. But the Frenchman remained in the cockpit though he never offered to spell Blessington at the wheel. The man drove Blessington to drink. He poured more Demerara and dipped his finger in the bag of crystal. A pulse fluttered under his collarbone, fear, speed.

Eventually Freycinet went below. After half an hour, Gillian came topside, clothed this time, in cutoffs and a halter. The sea had picked up, and she nearly lost her balance on the ladder.

"Steady," said Blessington.

"Want a roofie, Liam?"

He laughed. "A roofie? What's that? Some kind of . . ."

Gillian finished the thought he had been too much of a prude to articulate.

"Some kind of blow job? Some kind of sex technique? No, dear, it's a medication."

"I'm on watch."

She laughed at him. "You're shit-faced is what you are."

"You know," Blessington said, "you ought not to tease Honoré. You'll make him paranoid."

"He's an asshole. As we say back home."

"That may be. But he's a very mercurial fella. I used to work with him."

"Mercurial? If you know he's so mercurial how come you brought him?"

"I didn't bring him," Blessington said. "He brought me. For my vaunted seamanship. And I came for the money. How about you?"

"I came on account of having my brains in my ass," she said, shaking her backside. "My talent, too. Did you know I was a barrel racer? I play polo, too. English or Western, man, you name it."

"English or Western?" Blessington asked.

"Forget it," she said. She frowned at him, smiled, frowned again. "You seem, well, scared."

"Ah," said Blessington, "scared? Yes, I am. Somewhat."

"I don't give a shit," she said.

"You don't?"

"You heard me," she said. "I don't care what happens. Why should I? Me with my talent in my ass. Where do I come in?"

"You shouldn't talk that way," Blessington said.

"Fuck you. You afraid I'll make trouble? I assure you I could make trouble like you wouldn't believe."

"I don't doubt it," Blessington said. He kept his eyes on the Pitons. His terror, he thought, probably encouraged her.

"Just between you and me, Liam, I have no fear of dying. I would just as soon be out here on this boat now as in my little comfy bed with my stuffed animals. I would just as soon be dead."

He took another sip of rum to wet his pipes for speech. "Why did you put the money in, then? Weren't you looking for a score?"

"I don't care about money," she said. "I thought it would be a kick. I thought it would be radical. But it's just another exercise in how everything sucks."

"Well," said Blessington, "you're right there."

She looked off at the twin mountains.

"They don't seem a bit closer than they did this morning."

"No. It's an upwind passage. Have to tack forever."

"You know what Nigel told me back on Canouan?"

"No," Blessington said.

"He told me not to worry about understanding things. He said understanding was weak and lame. He said you got to *overstand* things." She hauled herself and did the voice of a big St. Vincentian man saddling up a white bitch for the night, laying down wisdom. "You got to *overstand* it. *Overstand* it, right? Funny, huh."

"Maybe there's something in it," said Blessington.

"Rasta lore," she said. "Could be, man."

"Anyway, never despise what the natives tell you, that's what my aunt used to say. Even in America."

"And what was your aunt? A dope dealer?"

"She was a nun," Blessington said. "A missionary."

For a while Gillian sunned herself on the foredeck, halter off. But the sun became too strong and she crawled back to the cockpit.

"You ever think about how it is in this part of the world?" she asked him. "The Caribbean and around it? It's all suckin' stuff they got. Suckin' stuff, all goodies and no nourishment."

"What do you mean?"

"It's all turn-ons and illusion," she said. "Don't you think? Like coffee." She numbered items on the long fingers of her left hand. "Tobacco. Emeralds. Sugar. Cocaine. Ganja. It's all stuff you don't need. Isn't even good for you. Perks and pick-me-ups and pogy bait. Always has been."

"You're right," Blessington said. "Things people kill for."

"Overpriced. Put together by slaves and peons. Piggy stuff. For pink piggies."

"I hadn't thought of it," he said. He looked over at her. She had raised a fist to her pretty mouth. "You're clever, Gillian."

"You don't even like me," she said.

"Yes I do."

161

"What you're talking about, you two? About me, eh?"

"Damn, Honoré!" Gillian said. "He was just proposing." When he had turned around again she spoke between her teeth. "Shithead is into the blow. He keeps prying up the sole. Cures Marie's mal de mer. Keeps him on his toes."

"God save us," said Blessington. Leaning his elbow on the helm he took Gillian's right hand and put it to her forehead, her left shoulder and then her right one, walking through the sign of the cross. "Pray for us like a good girl."

Gillian made the sign again by herself. "Shit," she said, "now I feel a lot better. No, really," she said when he laughed, "I do. I'm gonna do it all the time now. Instead of chanting, *Om* or *Nam myoho renge kyo.*"

164   They sat and watched the peaks grow closer, though the contrary current increased.

"When this is over," Blessington said, "maybe we ought to stay friends."

"If we're still alive," she said, "we might hang out together. We could go to your restaurant in the Keys."

"That's what we'll do," he said. "I'll make you a sous-chef."

"I'll wait tables."

"No, no. Not you."

"But we won't be alive," she said.

"But if we are."

"If we are," she said, "we'll stay together." She looked at him sway beside the wheel. "You better not be shitting me."

"I wouldn't. I think it was meant to be."

"Meant to be? You're putting me on."

"Don't make me weigh my words, Gillian. I want to say what occurs to me."

"Right," she said, touching him. "When we're together you can say any damn thing."

The green mountains, in the full richness of afternoon, rose above them. Blessington had a look at the chart to check the location of the offshore reefs. He began steering to another quarter, away from the tip of the island.

Gillian sat on a locker with her arms around his neck leaning against his back. She smelled of sweat and patchouli.

"I've never been with anyone as beautiful as you, Gillian."

He saw she had gone to sleep. He disengaged her arms and helped her lie flat on the locker in the shifting shade of the mainsail. Life is a dream, he thought. Something she knew and I didn't.

I love her, Blessington thought. She encourages me. The shadow of the peaks spread over the water.

Freycinet came out on deck and called up to him.

"Liam! We're to stop here. Off les Pitons."

"We can't," Blessington said, though it was tempting. He was so tired.

"We have to stop. We can anchor, yes? Marie is sick. We need to rest. We want to see them."

"We'd have to clear customs," Blessington said. "We'll have bloody cops and boat boys and God knows what else."

He realized at once what an overnight anchorage would entail. All of them up on speed or the cargo, cradling shotguns, peering into the moonlight while they waited for *macheteros* to come on feathered oars and steal their shit and kill them.

He gave Blessington the wheel, then he took Gillian under the arm and pulled her up out of the cockpit. "Get below! I don't want to fucking see you." He followed her below and Blessington heard him speak briefly to Marie. The young woman began to moan. The Pitons looked close enough to strike with a rock and a rich jungle smell came out on the wind. Freycinet, back on deck, looked as though he was sniffing out menace. A divi-divi bird landed on the boom for a moment and then fluttered away.

"I think I have a place," Blessington said, "if you still insist. A reef."

"A reef, eh?"

"A reef about four thousand meters offshore."

"We could have a swim, *non?*"

"We could, yes."

"But I don't know if I want to swim with you, Liam. I think you try to push me overboard."

"I think I saved your life," Blessington said.

They motored on to the reef with Freycinet standing in the bow to check for bottom as Blessington watched the depth recorder. At ten meters of bottom, they were an arm's length from the single float in view. Blessington cut the engine and came about and then went forward to cleat a line to the float. The float was painted red, yellow and green, Rasta colors like Gillian's bracelet.

It was late afternoon and suddenly dead calm. The protection the Pitons offered from the wind was ideal and the bad current that ran over the reef to the south seemed to divide around these coral heads. A perfect dive site, Blessington thought, and he could not understand why even in June there were not more floats or more boats anchored there. It seemed a steady enough place even for an overnight anchorage, although the cruising guide advised against it because of the dangerous reefs on every side.

The big ketch lay motionless on unruffled water; the float line drifted slack. There was sandy beach and a palm-lined shore across the water. It was a lonely part of the coast, across a jungle mountain track from the island's most remote resort. Through binoculars Blessington could make out a couple of boats hauled up on the strand but no one seemed ready to come out and hustle them. With luck it was too far from shore.

It might be also, he thought, that for metaphysical reasons the *Sans Regret* presented a forbidding aspect. But an aspect that deterred small predators might in time attract big ones.

Marie came up, pale and hollow-eyed, in her bikini. She gave Blessington a chastising look and lay down on the cushions on the afterdeck. Gillian came up behind her and took a seat on the gear locker behind Blessington.

"The fucker's got no class," she said softly. "See him hit me?"

"Of course. I was next to you."

"Gonna let him get away with that?"

"Well," Blessington said, "for the moment it behooves us to let him feel in charge."

"Behooves us?" she asked. "You say it *behooves* us?"

"That's right."

"Hey, what were you gonna do back there, Liam?" she asked. "Deep-six him?"

"I honestly don't know. He might have fallen."

"I was wondering," she said. "He was wondering, too."

"Everyone all right? asked Blessington.

"Fucking monkeys!" Freycinet swore.

"Well," Blessington said, watching the boat disappear, "they're gone for now. Maybe," he suggested to Freycinet, "we can have our swim and go, too."

Freycinet looked at him blankly as though he had no idea what Blessington was on about. He nodded vaguely.

After half an hour Marie rose and stood on the bulwark and prepared to dive, arms foremost. When she went, her dive was a good one, straight-backed and nearly splash-free. She performed a single stroke underwater and sped like a bright shaft between the coral heads below and the crystal surface. Then she appeared prettily in the light of day, blinking like a child, shaking her shining hair.

From his place in the bow, Freycinet watched Marie's dive, her underwater career, her pert surfacing. His expression was not affectionate but taut and tight-lipped. The muscles in his neck stood out, his moves were twitchy like a street junkie's. He looked exhausted and angry. The smell of cordite hovered around him.

"He's a shithead and a loser," Gillian said softly to Blessington. She looked not at Freycinet but toward the green mountains. "I thought he was cool. He was so fucking mean—I like respected that. Now we're all gonna die. Well," she said, "goes to show, right?"

"Don't worry," Blessington told her. "I won't leave you."

"Whoa," said Gillian. "All right!" But her enthusiasm was not genuine. She was mocking him.

Blessington forgave her.

Freycinet pointed a finger at Gillian. "Swim!"

"What if I don't wanna?" she asked, already standing up. When he began to swear at her in a hoarse voice she took her clothes off in front of them. Everything but the Rasta bracelet.

"I think I will if no one minds," she said. "Where you want me to swim to, Honoré?"

"Swim to fucking *Amérique*," he said. He laughed as though his mood had improved. "You want her, Liam?"

"People are always asking me that," Blessington said. "What do I have to do?"

"You swim to fucking *Amérique* with her."

Blessington saw Gillian take a couple of pills from her cutoff pocket and swallow them dry.

"I can't swim that far," Blessington said.

"Go as far as you can," said Freycinet.

"How about you?" Gillian said to the Frenchman. "You're the one wanted to stop. So ain't you gonna swim?"

"I don't trust her," Freycinet said to Blessington. "What do you think?"

"She's a beauty," Blessington said. "Don't provoke her."

Gillian measured her beauty against the blue water and dived over the side. A belly full of pills, Blessington thought. But her strokes when she surfaced were strong and defined. She did everything well, he thought. She was good around the boat. She had a pleasant voice for country music. He could imagine her riding, a cowgirl.

"Bimbo, eh?" Freycinet asked. "That's it, eh?"

"Yes," Blessington said. "Texas and all that."

"*Oui*," said Freycinet. "Texas." He yawned. "*Bien*. Have your swim with her. If you want."

Blessington went down into the stinking cabin and put his

173

Stoned and frightened as he was, he could not make sense of it, regain his perspective. He took a swig from a plastic bottle of warm Evian water, dropped his towel, and jumped overboard.

The water felt good, slightly cool. He could relax against it and slow the beating of his heart. It seemed to cleanse him of the cabin stink. He was at home in the water, he thought. Marie was frolicking like a mermaid, now close to the boat. Gillian had turned back and was swimming toward him. Her stroke still looked strong and accomplished; he set out to intercept her course.

They met over a field of elkhorn coral. Some of the formations were so close to the surface that their feet, treading water, brushed the velvety skin of algae over the sharp prongs.

"How are you?" Blessington asked her.

She had a lupine smile. She was laughing, looking at the boat. Her eyes appeared unfocused, the black pupils huge under the blue glare of afternoon and its shimmering crystal reflection. She breathed in hungry swallows. Her face was raw and swollen where Freycinet had hit her.

"Look at that asshole," she said, gasping.

Freycinet was standing on deck talking to Marie, who was in the water ten feet away. He held a mask and snorkel in one hand and a pair of swim fins in the other. One by one he threw the toys into the water for Marie to retrieve. He looked coy and playful.

Something about the scene troubled Blessington, although he could not, in his state, quite reason what it was. He watched Freycinet take a few steps back and paw the deck like an angry bull. In the next moment, Blessington realized what the problem was.

"Oh, Jesus Christ," he said.

Freycinet leaped into space. He still wore the greasy shorts he had worn on the whole trip. In midair he locked his arms around his bent knees. He was holding a plastic spatula in his right hand. He hit the surface like a cannonball, raising a little waterspout, close enough to Marie to make her yelp.

"You know what?" Gillian asked. She had spotted it. She was amazing.

"Yes, I do. The ladder's still up. We forgot to lower it,"

"Shit," she said and giggled.

Blessington turned over to float on his back and tried to calm himself. Overhead the sky was utterly cloudless. Moving his eyes only a little he could see the great green tower of Gros Piton, shining like Jacob's ladder itself, thrusting toward the empty blue. Incredibly far above, a plane drew out its jet trail, a barely visible needle stitching the tiniest flaw in the vast perfect seamless curtain of day. Miles and miles above, beyond imagining.

"How we gonna get aboard?" Gillian asked. He did not care for the way she was acting in the water now, struggling to stay afloat, moving her arms too much, wasting her breath.

"We'll have to go up the float line. Or maybe," he said, "we can stand on each other's shoulders."

"I'm not," she said, gasping, "gonna like that too well."

"Take it easy, Gillian. Lie on your back."

What bothered him most was her laughing, a high-pitched giggle with each breath.

"Okay, let's do it," she said, spitting salt water. "Let's do it before he does."

"Slow and steady," Blessington said.

They slowly swam together, breaststroking toward the boat. A late-afternoon breeze had come up as the temperature began to fall.

Freycinet and Marie had allowed themselves to drift farther and farther from the boat. Blessington urged Gillian along beside him until the big white hull was between them and the other swimmers.

Climbing was impossible. It was partly the nature of the French-made boat: an unusually high transom and the rounded glassy hull made it particularly difficult to board except from a dock or a dinghy. That was the contemporary, security-conscious style. And the rental company had removed a few of the deck fittings that might have provided hand- and footholds. Still, he tried to find a grip so that Gillian could get on his shoulders. Once he even managed to position himself between her legs and push her a foot or so up the hull, as she sat on his shoulders. But there was nothing to grab and she was stoned. She swore and laughed and toppled off him.

He was swimming forward along the hull, looking for the float, when it occurred to him suddenly that the boat must be moving. Sure enough, holding his place, he could feel the hull sliding to windward under his hand. In a few strokes he was under the bow, feeling the ketch's weight thrusting forward, riding him down. Then he saw the Rastafarian float. It was unencumbered by any line. Honoré and Marie had not drifted from the boat—the boat itself was slowly blowing away, accompanied now by the screech of fiberglass against coral, utterly unsecured. The boys from the Pitons, having dealt with druggies before, had undone the mooring line while they were sleeping or nodding off or scarfing other sorts of lines.

Blessington hurried around the hull, with one hand to the boat's skin, trying to find the drifting float line. It might, he thought, be possible to struggle up along that. But there was no drifting float line. The boat boys must have uncleated it and balled the cleat in nylon line and silently tossed it aboard. They had been so feckless, the sea so glassy, and the wind so low that the big boat had simply settled on the float, with its keel fast among the submerged elkhorn, and they had imagined themselves secured. The *Sans Regret*, to which he clung, was gone. Its teak interiors were in another world now, as far away as the tiny jet miles above them on its way to Brazil.

"It's no good," Blessington said to her.

"It's not?" She giggled.

"Please," he said, "please don't do that."

She gasped. "What?"

"Never mind," he said. "Come with me."

They had just started to swim away when a sudden breeze 179 carried the *Sans Regret* from between the two couples, leaving Blessington and Gillian and Honoré and Marie to face one another in the water across a distance of twenty yards or so. Honoré and Marie stared at their shipmates in confusion. It was an embarrassing moment. Gillian laughed.

"What have you done?" Honoré asked Blessington. Blessington tried not to look at him.

"Come on," he said to Gillian. "Follow me."

Cursing in French, Freycinet started kicking furiously for the boat. Marie, looking very serious, struck out behind him. Gillian stopped to look after them.

Blessington glanced at his diver's watch. It was five-fifteen.

"Never mind them," he said. "Don't look at them. Stay with me."

He turned over on his back and commenced an artless

backstroke, arms out straight, rowing with his palms, paddling with his feet. It was the most economic stroke he knew, the one he felt most comfortable with. He tried to make the strokes controlled and rhythmic rather than random and splashy to avoid conveying any impression of panic or desperation. To free his mind, he tried counting the strokes. As soon as they were over deep water, he felt the current. He tried to take it at a 45-degree angle, determining his bearing and progress by the great mountain overhead.

"Are you all right?" he asked Gillian. He raised his head to have a look at her. She was swimming in what looked like a good strong crawl. She coughed from time to time.

"I'm cold," she said. "That's the trouble."

"Try resting on your back," he said, "and paddling with your open hands. Like you were rowing."

She turned over and closed her eyes and smiled.

"I could go to sleep."

"You'll sleep ashore," he said. "Keep paddling."

They heard Freycinet cursing. Marie began to scream over and over again. It sounded fairly far away.

Checking on the mountain, Blessington felt a rush of despair. The lower slopes of the jungle were turning dark green. The line dividing sun-bright vegetation from deep-shaded green was withdrawing toward the peak. And the mountain looked no closer. He felt as though they were losing distance, being carried out faster than they could paddle. Marie's relentless screeches went on and on. Perhaps they were actually growing closer, Blessington thought, perhaps an evening tide was carrying them out.

"Poor kid," Gillian said. "Poor little baby."

"Don't listen," he said.

Gillian kept coughing, sputtering. He stopped asking her if she was all right.

"I'm sorry," she said. "I'm really cold now. I thought the water was warm at first."

"We're almost there," he said.

Gillian stopped swimming and looked up at Gros Piton. Turning over again to swim, she got a mouthful of water.

"Like . . . hell," she said.

"Keep going, Gillian."

It seemed to him, as he rowed the sodden vessel of his body and mind, that the sky was darkening. The sun's mark withdrew higher on the slopes. Marie kept screaming. They heard splashes far off where the boat was now. Marie and Honoré were clinging to it.

"Liam," Gillian said, "you can't save me."

"You'll save yourself," he said. "You'll just go on."

"I can't."

"Don't be a bloody stupid bitch."

"I don't think so," she said. "I really don't."

He stopped rowing himself then, although he was loath to. Every interruption of their forward motion put them more at the mercy of the current. According to the cruise book it was only a five-knot current but it felt much stronger. Probably reinforced by a tide.

Gillian was struggling, coughing in fits. She held her head up, greedy for air, her mouth open like a baby bird's in hope of nourishment. Blessington swam nearer her. The sense of their time ticking away, of distance lost to the current, enraged him.

"You've got to turn over on your back," he said gently. "Just ease onto your back and rest there. Then arch your back. Let your head lie backward so your forehead's in the water."

Trying to do as he told her, she began to thrash in a tangle of her own arms and legs. She swallowed water, gasped. Then she laughed again.

"Don't," he whispered.

"Liam? Can I rest on you?"

He stopped swimming toward her.

"You mustn't. You mustn't touch me. We mustn't touch each other. We might . . ."

"Please," she said.

"No. Get on your back. Turn over slowly."

Something broke the water near them. He thought it was the fin of a blacktip shark. A troublesome shark but not among the most dangerous. Of course, it could have been anything. Gillian still had the Rasta bracelet around her wrist.

"This is the thing, Liam. I think I got a cramp. I'm so dizzy."

"On your back, love. You must. It's the only way."

"No," she said. "I'm too cold. I'm too dizzy."

"Come on," he said. He started swimming again. Away from her.

"I'm so dizzy. I could go right out."

In mounting panic, he reversed direction and swam back toward her.

"Oh, shit," she said. "Liam?"

"I'm here."

"I'm fading out, Liam. I'll let it take me."

"Get on your back," he screamed at her. "You can easily swim. If you have to swim all night."

"Oh, shit," she said. Then she began to laugh again. She raised the hand that had the Rasta bracelet and splashed a sign of the cross.

"*Nam*," she said, "*Nam myoho renge kyo*. Son of a bitch." Laughing. What she tried to say next was washed out of her mouth by a wave.

"I can just go out," she said. "I'm so dizzy."

Then she began to struggle and laugh and cry.

"Praise God, from whom all blessings flow," she sang, laughing. "Praise him, all creatures here below."

"Gillian," he said. "For God's sake." Maybe I can take her in, he thought. But that was madness and he kept his distance.

She was laughing and shouting at the top of her voice.

"Praise him above, you heavenly host! Praise Father, Son, and Holy Ghost."

Laughing, thrashing, she went under, her face straining, wide-eyed. Blessington tried to look away but it was too late. He was afraid to go after her.

He lost his own balance then. His physical discipline collapsed and he began to wallow and thrash as she had.

"Help!" he yelled piteously. He was answered by a splash and Marie's screaming. Perhaps now he only imagined them.

Eventually he got himself under control. When the entire mountain had subsided into dark green, he felt the pull of the current release him. The breakers were beginning to carry him closer to the sand, toward the last spit of sandy beach remaining on the island. The entire northern horizon was subsumed in the mountain overhead, Gros Piton.

He had one final mad moment. Fifty yards offshore, a riptide was running; it seized him and carried him behind the tip of the island. He had just enough strength and coherence of mind to swim across it. The sun was setting as he waded out, among sea grape and manchineel. When he turned he could see against the setting sun the bare poles of the *Sans Regret*, settled on the larger reef to the south of the island. It seemed to him also that he could make out a struggling human figure, dark against the light hull. But the dark came down quickly. He thought he detected a flash of green. Sometimes he thought he could still hear Marie screaming.

All night, as he rattled through the thick brush looking for a road to follow from concealment, Gillian's last hymn echoed in his mind's ear. He could see her dying face against the black fields of sugarcane through which he trudged.

Once he heard what he was certain was the trumpeting of an elephant. It made him believe, in his growing delirium, that he was in Africa—Africa, where he had never been. He hummed the hymn. Then he remembered he had read somewhere that the resort maintained an elephant in the bush. But he did not want to meet it so he decided to stay where he was and wait for morning. All night he talked to Gillian, joked and sang hymns with her. He saved her again and again and they were together.

In the morning, when the sun rose fresh and full of promise, he set out for the Irish bar in Soufrière. He thought that they might overstand him there.

THE OCEAN *by* FREDERICK REIKEN

FREDERICK REIKEN (b. 1966) is the author of two novels, The Odd Sea, *which won the Hackney Literary Award for First Fiction, and the national bestseller* The Lost Legends of New Jersey. *In "The Ocean," published in* The New Yorker *in 2002, an adolescent boy and his marine biologist father spend the summer on the Caribbean island of St. John, where, among mangrove swamps and coral reefs, they both must face fears, love, and loss.*

ARLY THAT SUMMER, Dara and I were sitting on the rocky, volcanic tip of Yawzi Point. We were spying on Dara's mother, who was diving with a graduate student, Charles, on the reef a hundred feet below us. Charles was on St. John doing his own research, on gorgonian sea fans, but he sometimes helped professors gather data. Dara thought Charles and her mother might be having an affair

Dara asked me whether my father ever dated his students. "Sometimes," I said. "Although that was before he met Beverly."

"Were they voluptuous?" Dara asked.

I said one was.

"My mother says that men like younger women to be voluptuous, but younger men like older women to be skinny and athletic."

"I never heard that," I said, just as the sky rumbled with thunder. The rain came in over the bay, changing the color of the water from turquoise to dark blue. Dara yelled, "Mangoes!" and we ran to the grove.

As the rain fell we waited by a mango tree. Picking the mangoes was forbidden because everything in that part of St. John was national parkland. Nothing could be disturbed. That meant the mangoes, iguanas, conches, and all the coral on the reef. But we found ways around the rules—such as rainstorms that knocked mangoes from the mango trees. I glanced at Dara. She smiled mischievously. "Whoops," Dara said, and hit a tree limb with her shoulder. "Oops," I said, and shook another limb. We used our dripping wet shirts as pouches to hold the mangoes and quickly took them to Dara's bungalow.

I was thirteen. Dara was fourteen. She was from Utah and knew how to get moray eels to eat out of her hand. Her mother was doing research on the territoriality of damselfish. She was tenured at a university in Salt Lake City. Like my father, she was teaching marine biology at the School for Field Studies that summer.

Dara had blond hair that the Caribbean sun turned white. I loved the way her face looked underwater. Her eyes would seem very expressive, but with her mouth around her regulator she smiled in a way that my father said was "languid." I also liked the way she would point to barracudas and then nervously give me the O.K. sign. Dara was constantly giving me the O.K. sign underwater.

Once, we buddy-breathed at fifty feet, and that night Dara

said she'd felt like we were kissing underwater. On another dive we landed on a stingray. When our fins touched on the seafloor, the sand moved and we both kicked up as a giant stingray flapped away. Dara turned quickly and gave me the O.K. sign. I took my slate, wrote, "Holy fuck!" and held it before her eyes. She smiled and wrote, "Holy fucking fuck!" on her slate. I was about to write, "Holy fucking fucking fuck" when Dara swam up close and pressed her mask to mine. For a few seconds we stared with our eyes an inch apart. Then she pulled her head back and gave me the O.K. sign. On her slate she wrote, "I wanted to see the color of your eyes."

FROM DARA'S BUNGALOW that night we could hear soldier crabs in the forest—a loud *whooshing* that sounded more like wind than like crabs. Dara's mother was sitting on her bed with Charles, playing gin rummy and eating the stolen mangoes. Charles was talking about himself, as usual, going on about the English countryside, where he lived. He took out a cigarette and lit it, maybe because he knew the smell of smoke would make us leave.

Outside we caught two soldier crabs, which was easy, though it went against park rules. We took the crabs to my father's and my bungalow, but my father was there, sitting at his small desk with a pile of slates. "Professor Kahn, what are you doing?" Dara asked him. He told Dara he was grading the underwater-identification quiz he'd given to his students that afternoon. He said that no one had identified the tunicate *Ascidia nigra*, which is a black piece of slime that lives on rocks. My father often pointed it out while we were snorkeling. He liked informing people that *Ascidia nigra* was, evolutionarily, our closest relative on the reef.

My father's hair had grown back after he'd been bald for three months, from chemotherapy. Now he was in remission from his leukemia. He'd grown a beard for the first time, and it made him look like Grizzly Adams. He said, "Ten points if you can tell me the taxonomic classification for those hermit crabs?" Dara guessed *Uca*, which was wrong. That was the fiddler crab. I said, "It's *Coenobita clypeatus*." He said, "Ten points! Now please go set Mr. and Mrs. Clypeatus free."

We took the crabs back to the woods behind Dara's bungalow, where Dara's mother and Charles were still playing gin rummy. Charles's nasally British accent made me think of "Monty Python's Flying Circus." "It's my mist-aaaake!" I sang to Dara, who stared back blankly. "It's Monty Python," I said. "One of their gag lines."

We took turns lying down and letting Mr. and Mrs. Clypeatus walk around on our backs and stomachs. This got us both all sandy, so we decided to go swimming in the bay called Little Lameshur. It's pronounced La-muh-shoor and we sometimes joked about this name. I said, "You sure?" and Dara answered, "Lameshur."

At the beach we took our shirts off. I wondered whether Dara would take her bra off. I wondered why she wore a bra at all. We heard hooves clomping and turned in time to see a herd of feral donkeys. In the moonlight they seemed like phantom creatures. They trotted into the eucalyptus forest behind the road.

188

I told Dara that my father thought the donkeys could be studied by a biologist who was interested in equid sociality. They had harems, my father said, which meant that males had groups of females that they fought for or guarded territory for. That was what some Ph.D. candidate would have to figure out.

Dara said, "Hey, you know, there's an opening at the college where my mother works. My mom's on the search committee. Maybe your father could apply."

"What's the course load?" This was a question that my father would have asked.

"I don't know," Dara said. "All I know is that they've been searching since last fall."

"He might apply," I said, "although he likes his job at Rutgers. He'd also have to make sure that he was better."

"Better than who?" she asked.

I hadn't told her yet about my father's illness.

I said, "Just better. He had leukemia last winter."

She pressed her balled up shirt against her chin and seemed embarrassed.

"He doesn't seem sick," she said.

"Right now he's not. He was treated with chemotherapy."

Dara said, "Oh," and stopped talking about the job opening in Utah. That always happened when I mentioned my father's illness. People stopped talking.

I said, "He's been in remission since February."

Dara nodded.

I said, "People don't always die from it."

Dara said, "Oh."

"Should we go swimming?"

She dropped her shirt in the sand and took her bra off. I'd been thinking that I wanted to kiss her, but I could tell she was still thinking about my father.

It was low tide, and Little Lameshur had a sandbar. We had to walk before we got to water that was deep enough to swim in. I took her hand. "I found a sand dollar here," she said, "but it disintegrated."

I said, "That always happens with sand dollars." I considered this our first official conversation while holding hands.

When we got to chest-high water we dived in. After we swam around I got up the nerve to ask Dara if I could kiss her. She said yes, so I slid my arms around her waist. "Are you O.K.?" she asked, because I'd started shivering. "A little cold," I said, and kissed her. Her lips tasted like salt water. "Do that again," Dara said. We continued kissing for a while and then just hugged as we stood there in the ocean. I noticed other things—a rising half moon and stars reflected on the blue-black surface of the water. There were no boats, no islands, no light except the moon. I was afraid for a few seconds, and then I wasn't. When we were back on the beach we kissed again, and I wondered what I had been scared of.

ON JULY 4TH, my father took me snorkeling in the mangroves, which smell disgusting—like very rotten eggs. But the mangrove swamp functions like a nursery. It's where all sorts of juvenile creatures live before they're big enough to survive out on the reef. My father said he had seen lemon sharks and nurse sharks the size of a lobster. He had seen lobsters that were only slightly bigger than his thumb. While we were walking there, I told him about the job opening in Utah. I said I didn't know the course load but Dara's mom could probably pull strings for him. I said that Utah might be nicer than Piscataway, where we lived, that there'd be ski mountains nearby and maybe lots of beautiful blond people like Dara and her mother. My father said he had no plans to change jobs right now and certainly no plans ever to live in Utah

"What's wrong with Utah?" I asked.

He seemed flustered and said, "Nothing's wrong with Utah. Except it's far away and right now it's the last . . ."

He put both hands on his head, the way football coaches do when their kicker misses an easy field goal.

"It's the last what?"

"The last thing I have time to think about," he said.

"Why?"

He took his hands down and said, "Jordan, we need to talk about some things. Let's take our snorkel and then we'll have a conversation."

Once we were actually swimming in the mangroves, I stopped noticing the sulfury rotten-egg smell. Swimming was tricky because the roots made an underwater maze. They were encrusted with algae, sponges, anemones, and barnacles. Schools of young reef fish swam around them. We also saw some tiny crabs and lobsters, but no sharks. Each time I picked up my head and looked around, I was reminded that we were swimming under a forest. Above the water the mangrove roots made giant chairlike shapes that you could sit on. After we'd snorkeled for a while we climbed up onto one to have our conversation.

He began by mentioning that a few months ago he wasn't even sure if he'd be well enough to teach a class this summer. Did I understand that his health was still a thing he had to be concerned about? I said I did. He started talking about Beverly, his girlfriend. She'd be arriving in St. John in three weeks. He said he wanted to discuss something hypothetical. "About Beverly?" I asked, and he said yes, it had to do with Beverly. Then he asked whether, in the event that his illness recurred and he was not able to get better, it would be O.K. if Beverly adopted me.

"If you were dead, you mean?" I asked.

"That's what I mean."

He'd been with Beverly three years, ever since we moved from Rhode Island to New Jersey. She was a divorced pediatrician with two daughters. I'd been to her house in East Brunswick a few times and liked Rocky, her younger daughter, who was in the same grade as me. Her older daughter, Jennifer, always seemed angry and I hadn't ever talked to her. But she had seashells all over her bedroom, which made me think there was a chance I'd like her, too.

I said, "I guess it would be fine."

"I'm glad to hear that," he said. "Beverly loves you."

We had our masks on our heads and our fins rested against the long roots of the mangrove. My father's beard was all wet. It had a gray patch that reminded me of coral. His wavy, sun-bleached hair was bunched up above his mask.

"I'd like to tell you something about your mother," he said.

"O.K.," I said. My mother died when I was six, when she was driving home from a supermarket in Providence. She was hit by someone going the wrong way on the highway's off ramp. Whenever Dad talked about Mom, it made me anxious.

He said, "I once brought her down here for the summer. That was in 1964, when I was studying long-spined urchins for my doctorate."

I said, "They're black. *Diadema antillarum.*"

He said, "That's right."

"I saw some in Little Lameshur."

"They're everywhere," he said. "But I'm not talking about sea urchins."

"So what do you want to tell me?"

He said, "Your mother and I, we once sat right here in these mangroves."

"This exact tree?"

"Maybe."

"It would be neat if it was actually this tree."

"It might have been." He looked at me. "Your mother and I were young and very happy. We were just sitting in these mangroves."

I said, "O.K.," and nodded, trying to act like I was getting what he was saying. Then I said, "Dad, do you think you will die?"

He said, "It's possible."

"But you said people survive leukemia."

"Some people do," he said. "More often, it comes back."

to his eyes. "It's almost two," he said. "How do you feel about going down to Big Lameshur for a night dive? We could be back here by four and sleep for a few more hours."

My father had never taken me on a night dive. I asked him if we could use Cyalume sticks. They have a liquid inside that glows fluorescent green after you hit them. He said we'd wear them on our weight belts.

We only went down thirty feet, but even at that depth we saw things that you usually can't see during the day. A spotted moray was crawling along the bottom. A queen angelfish seemed to be resting in the space beneath a head of brain coral. Its eyes were open but it wasn't moving. It was as if it was just sitting in the water. Then, as we swam around the head of coral, I saw a shark-shaped shadow lying on the seafloor. My father shined his underwater light on it. A nurse shark. Full grown. It was yellowish brown, with spots. It had two dorsal fins and barbels hanging from its nostrils, like a catfish. I knew that nurse sharks weren't aggressive, but I was panicking and I pointed to the surface. My father gave me the O.K. sign, took my arm, and we started our ascent.

One of the "Seven Rules of Diving" was "Go up slowly." "Stop, think, then act" was another—though I definitely didn't think before I acted. When we broke through the water's surface, I began kicking madly with my flippers. I didn't stop until I reached the shallow water by the dock. When Dad caught up, I was crouching in the water.

"It was a nurse shark," he said. "They aren't dangerous."

I said, "I know."

He said, "Then what were you afraid of?"

"It was so big."

He said, "You swam with manatees in Florida. They're much bigger."

I told him, "Manatees aren't sharks."

He crouched next to me. A damselfish was nipping at my ankle. My father liked to tell his students that the damselfish were by far the most aggressive fish on the reef.

He said, "You know, I've swum with mako sharks and tiger sharks in Australia. I once swam right through fifty or more blue sharks that had gathered near a sandbar in Bermuda. Even the great white shark I saw in the South Seas left me alone."

"Weren't you ever scared?" I asked.

He shook his head and said, "Whenever I'm in the water, I feel safe."

197

We climbed up onto the dock, took off our tanks and our BCs, and sat listening to the water. The knot in my stomach slowly came loose, and in the faint light I looked out toward the spot where we'd been diving. The funny thing was that I'd always wanted to see a nurse shark.

I MADE A NECKLACE FOR DARA out of a Cyalume stick and a piece of string. The night she wore it we walked out to the sugar-mill ruins to see Sammy, an old mongoose who lived under the foundation. She wore it backward. I let her walk ahead of me and all I could see was the greenish-yellow glow.

We drank the rum again, but we got caught. Dara's mom smelled it on her breath when she got back to the bungalow.

creature. It had a polished black-and-caramel-colored shell and a curved beak. It swam away fast, flapping its legs like it was flying. Later that night, lying in bed, I kept imagining us holding hands and following the turtle.

THEY WERE SCREWING, DARA SAID. And it was possible. I'd seen my father telephone Beverly after dinner, like he always did. Then he and Julia vanished. We checked the bungalows and every one of the classrooms. They weren't anywhere.

I said, "They might be just sitting on the beach somewhere. They could be talking about *Rhodactis*."

"My mom's a slut," Dara said. She walked away from me and bent down on the volleyball court. She was picking up a stone. She said, "My mother will screw anyone she can."

"What does your father say?"

"He does it, too. It's not such a good marriage."

She kept picking up stones and throwing them through the volleyball net. I heard them hitting the ground on the other side.

"Let's get a mango," I said.

"Sometimes I hate my mother's guts."

"She seems O.K.," I said.

"Do you hate your father?"

I said, "No."

Dara kept staring at me, as if it was so strange that I liked my father.

I said, "How come your parents aren't seeing a therapist?"

"It wouldn't help much."

"How do you know?"

She said, "I know."

"My dad and his girlfriend, Beverly, see a therapist. They started going when he got sick."

"My parents aren't sick," Dara said. "Their only problem is that they're idiots."

"But still, a therapist could help them with their marriage—"

"Just leave me alone!" she yelled. "You stupid boy."

She walked away and went into her bungalow.

I yelled, "You're weird!" but followed anyway. There were no locks on the doors, so I walked right in. Dara was sitting at the foot of her bed, her arms crossed, looking as if she was in pain.

I said, "Let's not talk anymore about our parents."

She said, "You're right, I'm weird like you. I'm also angry."

"At who?"

"What?"

"Who are you angry at? You just said that you're angry."

"God, you're so dense," Dara said. She took my arm and pulled me down so I was sitting right beside her. I tried to kiss her, but she suddenly started crying. I asked, "What's wrong?" and she said, "My life." I asked her what was so bad about her life. She said her boyfriend Kyle had dumped her for an anorexic cheerleader. She said her father had been in Texas since late winter and her parents had been talking about divorce.

When she stopped crying we went outside. It was dusk. We walked for a long time—past Little Lameshur, and all the way down the path that led to Europa Bay. I'd only been there by

After two more nosebleeds, he decided he should stop diving for a while. He said he needed to heal his nasal vessels. Almost incredibly, Julia and Beverly kept going out, the two of them. "Adults are strange" became Dara's recurring comment.

At night they'd all sit in the classroom and go over the new data. Dara called this their "*Rhodactis* ménage à trois." Once, we snuck up to the window and crouched, listening. We heard my father ask a riddle. What did one vulture say to the other? He told the answer—"Carry on"—and then Julia asked him how he was feeling. He said, "Not bad. So far there isn't any reason to leave the island."

A few days later, I caught my father holding hands with Julia. I'd gone to look for him in his classroom after his students had come out. When I walked in they were standing with their hands clasped. They pulled their hands apart but didn't seem concerned that I had caught them.

Dara was in a good mood that day. She'd gone out snorkeling in Big Lameshur by herself, although technically you should always have a buddy. She had discovered a small inlet full of fanworms. They look like colorful fans or feathers and live in coral. Later that afternoon, she took me to her secret inlet. We swam over the fanworms and dived down to touch them and make them pull their feathers in. One type of fanworm looks just like a tiny Christmas tree. I started thinking about Christmas and wondered whether my father would be alive then. I also had a thought that didn't make much sense but still seemed logical. I thought that somehow, in the ocean, we stay connected to everything that's dead.

It was a hot day and very muggy. We swam back behind some rocks, where it was shallow. Dara unzipped her shorty wetsuit and peeled it down to her waist. She had a bathing suit underneath, and she slid the straps down off her shoulders. The suit was white and almost see-through and it looked sexy. She said, "Hey, big boy," and pulled her bathing suit down, too.

We took our masks and fins and all our clothes off. We piled everything up on one big rock. There was another rock that was even bigger, so we lay down on it and listened to that soft noise you can hear only when you're lying on rocks in a calm inlet beside the ocean.

"Sometimes I wish that we were older," I said.

Dara said nothing. She took my hand and kissed my knuckles.

I said, "I think we're in love, don't you? If we were older we could run away and live on some island just like this one."

Dara sat up after that, breathed deeply, and said, "Please don't make me cry."

"I wasn't trying to."

She kissed my hand again and said, "You always act so serious."

I said, "I'm serious and brooding. My mother used to tell me I was sullen—and so what?"

Dara smiled and said, "O.K., so we're in love a little, maybe. But I live in stupid Utah. And I don't plan to move to any islands. Don't get too mushy on me, O.K.?"

I said, "O.K."

After dinner that night, there was a movie, but it was still so hot that Dara and I decided to take another swim. I went to crouched so that our eyes were exactly level. She said, "This year might be very, very hard."

THE NEXT MORNING I woke to the sound of braying donkeys. One of them stood right outside, looking at me through the screen. "Someone please kill that thing," said Beverly. I had to pee, so I went outside and shooed him. He took two steps back and proceeded to bray his head off once again

I felt awake, and I told my dad and Beverly I was going to walk down to Little Lameshur. Dad mumbled, "Fine," though he was already half asleep again. It must have been about six o'clock, but the sun seemed hot, so I wore my tank top. I wandered out toward Little Lameshur and decided to walk the path to Yawzi Point.

It was the first time I'd been out there without Dara. I sat down on a rock that jutted out above the reef. The fire-coral welt on my chest still burned and I took my top off so the cool breeze would soothe it. A group of pelicans swam below me. They were fishing around the reef, and every now and then one of them would dive under. They sometimes twisted their necks so far that when they surfaced they would be swimming in the opposite direction. I watched one tilt back its head to swallow a fish that was still alive and flapping inside its throat pouch.

Two other pelicans crashed down and joined the others. I thought about the talk I'd had with Beverly, and somehow watching this group of pelicans seemed to be a way of getting ready. So did looking at the turquoise surface of the water. So did imagining everything beneath it. All the trumpetfish and damselfish and angelfish. The spotted moray eels and sea cucumbers and stingrays and barracudas. Ten feet beneath the water's surface, there were sea sponges in every different color you could imagine. There were bright-yellow-and-pink anemones and the emerald-green false coral *Rhodactis*. The more I thought the more I realized I could go on and on with all the things that lived inside the ocean.

Another pelican smashed into the water, and as I watched it land I got the urge to climb down the steep slope. One short stretch was almost vertical, and when I got down I wondered what I had been thinking. I wasn't going to be able to climb back up. The only way back was to swim to Little Lameshur. I leapt onto a big rock and saw a cavern of deep water just beyond it. A school of blue tang passed beneath me. I dived in.

Without a mask, everything was blurry. I kept my eyes open and saw vague shapes that were coral mounds and sponge formations ten or fifteen feet below me. It was slow going with my sneakers, but I kept swimming out to where it was too deep to see the bottom. I knew that nurse sharks and lemon sharks might be swimming underneath me. For all I knew, a great white shark was down there, but I kept holding my breath and kicking through the water, now and then looking up to see where the group of pelicans had gone.

THE HOTEL *by* ISAAC BASHEVIS SINGER

ISAAC BASHEVIS SINGER (1904–1991) was the first Yiddish writer to be awarded the Nobel Prize. Born in Poland, Singer immigrated to New York before World War II and, in 1973, bought an apartment in Miami, Florida. This gently comic portrait of Jewish émigrés in doctor-mandated retirement shows that Miami Beach may not be everyone's idea of paradise on earth.

WHEN ISRAEL DANZIGER RETIRED to Miami Beach it seemed to him as if he were retiring to the other world. At the age of fifty-six he had been compelled to abandon everything he had known: the factory in New York, his houses, the office, his children, his relatives, and his friends. Hilda, his wife, bought a house with a garden on the banks of Indian Creek. It had comfortable rooms on the ground floor, a patio, a swimming pool, palms, flower beds, a gazebo, and special chairs designed to put little strain on the heart. The creek stank a bit, but there was a cool breeze from the ocean just across the street.

The water was green and glassy, like a stage decoration at the opera, with white ships skimming over its surface. Seagulls squeaked shrilly above and swooped down to catch fish. On the white sands lay half-naked women. Israel Danziger did not need binoculars to view them; he could see them behind his sunglasses.

He could even hear their gabble and laughter.

He had no worries of being forgotten. They would all come down from New York in the winter to visit him—his sons, his daughters, and their in-laws. Hilda was already concerned about not having enough bedrooms and linen, and also that Israel might have too much excitement with all the visitors from the city. His doctor had prescribed complete rest.

It was September now, and Miami Beach was deserted. The hotels closed their doors, posting signs that they would reopen in December or January. In the cafeterias downtown, which only yesterday had swarmed with people, chairs were piled atop bare tables, the lights extinguished, and business at a standstill. The sun blazed, but the newspapers were full of warnings of a hurricane from some far-off island, admonishing their readers to prepare candles, water, and storm windows, although it was far from certain whether the hurricane would touch Miami. It might bypass Florida entirely and push out into the Atlantic.

The newspapers were bulky and boring. The same news items which stirred the senses in New York seemed dull and meaningless here. The radio programs were vacuous and television was idiotic. Even books by well-known writers seemed flat.

Israel still had an appetite, but Hilda carefully doled out his rations. Everything he liked was forbidden—full of cholesterol— butter, eggs, milk, coffee with cream, a piece of fat meat. Instead she filled him with cottage cheese, salads, mangoes, and orange juice, and even this was measured out to him by the ounce lest, heaven forbid, he might swallow a few extra calories.

Israel Danziger lay on a deck chair, clad only in swimming trunks and beach sandals. A fig tree cast its shadow over him; yet he still covered his bald pate with a straw cap. Without clothes, Israel Danziger wasn't Israel Danziger at all; he was just a little man, a bundle of skin and bones, with a single tuft of hair on his chest, protruding ribs, knobby knees, and arms like sticks. Despite all the suntan lotion he smeared on himself, his skin was covered with red blotches. Too much sun had inflamed his eyes.

He got up and immersed himself in the swimming pool, splashed around for a few minutes, and then climbed out again. He couldn't swim; all he did was dip himself, as if in a *mikvah*. Some weeks ago he had actually begun a book, but he couldn't finish it. Every day he read the Yiddish newspaper from beginning to end, including the advertisements.

212   He carried with him a pad and a pencil, and from time to time he would estimate how much he was worth. He added up the profits from his apartment houses in New York and the dividends earned by his stocks and bonds. And each time the result was the same. Even if he was to live to be a hundred, Israel Danziger would still have more than enough, and there'd even be plenty for his heirs. Yet he could never really believe it. How and when did he amass such a fortune? And what would he do during all the years he was still destined to live: sit in the deck chair and gaze up at the sky?

Israel Danziger wanted to smoke, but the doctor allowed him only two cigars a day, and even that might be harmful. To dull his appetite for tobacco and for food, Israel chewed unsweetened gum. He bent down, plucked a blade of grass, and studied it. Then his eyes wandered to an orange tree nearby. He wondered what he would have thought if someone in Parciewe, his hometown in Poland, had told him that one day he would own a house in America, with citrus and coconut trees on the shores of the Atlantic Ocean in a land of eternal summer. Now he had all this, but what was it worth?

SUDDENLY ISRAEL DANZIGER TENSED. He thought he heard the telephone ringing inside. A long-distance call from New York, perhaps? He got up to answer it, and realized it was just a cricket which made noise like a bell. No one ever called him here. Who would call him? When a man liquidates his business, he's like a corpse.

Israel Danziger looked around again. The sky was pale blue, without even a cloud-puff. A single bird flew high above him. Where was it flying? The women who earlier had lain in the sand were now in the ocean. Although the sea was as smooth as a lake, they jumped up and down as if there were waves. They were fat, ugly, and broad-shouldered. There was about them a selfishness that sickens the souls of men. And for such parasites men worked, weakened their hearts, and died before their times?

Israel had also driven himself beyond his strength. The doctors had warned him. Israel spat on the ground. Hilda was supposed to be a faithful wife, but just let him close his eyes and she'd have another husband within a year, and this time she'd pick a taller man . . .

But what was he to do? Build a synagogue where no one comes to pray? Have a Torah inscribed that nobody would read? Give away money to a kibbutz and help the atheists live in free love? You couldn't even give money to charity these days. For whatever purpose you gave, the money was eaten up by the secretaries, fundraisers, and politicians. By the time it was supposed to reach the needy, there was nothing left.

In the same notebook that Israel Danziger used to total up his income lay several letters which he had received only that morning. One from a yeshiva in Brooklyn, another from a Yiddish poet who was preparing to publish his work, a third from a home for the aged which wanted to build a new wing. The letters all sang the same refrain—send us a check. But what good would come from a few additional students at the yeshiva in Williamsburg? Who needed the poet's new verse? And why build a new wing? So that the president could arrange a banquet and take the cream off the milk? Perhaps the president was a builder himself, or he had a son-in-law who was an architect. I know that bunch, Israel Danziger grumbled to himself. They can't bluff me.

ISRAEL DANZIGER COULDN'T REMAIN SEATED any longer. He was engulfed by an emptiness as painful as any heart attack. The force that keeps men alive was draining from him and he knew without a doubt that he was only one step away from death, from madness. He had to do something immediately. He ran into his bedroom, flung open the doors of his closet, put on pants, a pair of socks, a shirt, a pair of shoes, then took up his cane and went out. His car was waiting in the garage, but he didn't want to drive a car and speed without purpose over the highway. Hilda was out shopping for groceries; the house would be empty, but no one stole things here. And did it matter if someone did try to break in? Besides, Joe the gardener was out tending the lawns, sprinkling water from a hose onto the bluish grass that had been brought here in sheets and now was spread over the sand like a carpet. Even the grass here has no roots, Israel Danziger thought. He envied Joe. At least that black man was doing something. He had a family somewhere near Miami.

What Israel Danziger was living through now was not mere boredom; it was panic. He had to act or perish. Maybe go to his broker and see how his stocks were getting along? But he'd already been there that morning for an hour. If he should take to going there twice a day, he would become a nuisance. Besides, it was twenty minutes to three. By the time he got there, they'd be closed.

The bus station was just across the street, and a bus was pulling up. Israel Danziger ran across the road, and this very act was like a drop of medicine. He climbed on the bus and threw in the coin. He'd go to Paprov's cafeteria. There he'd buy the afternoon paper, an exact duplicate of the morning paper, drink a cup of coffee, eat a piece of cake, smoke a cigar, and, who knows, perhaps he would meet someone he knew.

The bus was half empty. The passengers all sat on the shaded side and fanned themselves, some with fans, others with folded newspapers, and still others with the flaps of pocketbooks. Only one passenger sat on the side where the sun burned, a man who was beyond caring about heat. He looked unkempt, unshaven, and dirty. Must be drunk, Israel Danziger thought, and for the first time he understood drunkenness. He'd take a shot of whiskey, too, if he were allowed. Anything is better than this hollowness.

A passenger got off and Israel Danziger took his seat. A hot wind blew in through the open window. It tasted of the ocean, of half-melted asphalt and gasoline. Israel Danziger sat quietly. But

215

suddenly perspiration broke out over all his body and his fresh shirt was soaked in a second. He grew more cheerful. He reached the point where even a bus ride was an adventure.

On Lincoln Road were stores, shop windows, restaurants, banks. Newsboys were hawking papers. It was a little like a real city, almost like New York. Beneath one of the storefront awnings, Israel Danziger saw a poster advertising a big sale. The entire stock was to be sold. To Israel Danziger, Lincoln Road seemed like an oasis in the wilderness. He found himself worrying about the owners of the stores. How long would they hold out if they never saw a customer? He felt impelled to buy something, anything, to help business. It's a good deed, he told himself, better than giving to shnorrers.

The bus stopped, and Israel Danziger got off and entered the cafeteria. The revolving door, the air-conditioned chill, the bright lights burning in the middle of the day, the hubbub of customers, the clatter of dishes, the long steam tables laden with food and drink, the cashier ringing the cash register, the smell of tobacco—all this revived the spirit of Israel Danziger. He shook off his melancholy, his hypochondria and thoughts of death. With his right hand he grabbed a tray; his left hand he stuck into his rear pocket, where he had some bills and small change. He remembered his doctor's warnings, but a greater power—a power which makes the final decision—told him to go ahead. He bought a chopped-herring sandwich, a tall glass of iced coffee, and a piece of cheese cake. He lit a long cigar. He was Israel Danziger again, a living person, a businessman.

AT ANOTHER TABLE, across from Israel Danziger, sat a little man, no taller than Danziger but stocky, broad-shouldered, with a large head and a fat neck. He wore an expensive Panama hat (at least fifty dollars, Danziger figured), and a pink, short-sleeved shirt. On one of his fingers, plump as a sausage, a diamond glittered. He was puffing a cigar and leafing through a Yiddish newspaper, breaking off pieces from an egg pretzel. He removed his hat, and his bald head shone round and smooth. There was something childlike about his roundness, his fatness, and his puckered lips. He was not smoking his cigar; he was only sucking on it, and Israel Danziger wondered who he was. Certainly he was not a native. Perhaps a New Yorker? But what was he doing here in September, unless he suffered from hay fever? And, since he was reading a Yiddish paper, Israel Danziger knew he was one of the family. He wanted to get to know the man. For a while he hesitated; it wasn't like him to approach strangers. But here in Miami you can die of boredom if you're too reserved. He got up from his chair, took the plate with the cheese cake and the coffee, and moved over to the other man's table.

"Anything new in the paper?"

The man removed the cigar from his mouth. "What should be new? Nothing. Not a thing."

"In the old days there were writers, today scribblers," said Israel Danziger, just to say something.

"It's five cents wasted."

"What else can you do in Miami? It helps kill time."

"What are you doing here in this heat?"

"And what are you doing here?"

"It's my heart . . . I'm sitting around here six months already. The doctor exiled me here . . . I had to retire . . ."

"So—then we're brothers!" Israel Danziger exclaimed. "I have a heart too, a bad heart that gives me trouble. I got rid of everything in New York and my good wife bought me a house with fig trees, like in Palestine in the old days. I sit around and go crazy."

"Where is the house?"

Danziger told him.

"I pass it every day. I think I even saw you there once. What did you do before?"

Danziger told him.

"I myself have been in real estate for over thirty-five years," the other man said.

THE TWO MEN FELL INTO A CONVERSATION. The little man in the Panama hat said his name was Morris Sapirstone. He had an apartment on Euclid Avenue. Israel Danziger got up and bought two cups of coffee and two more egg pretzels. Then he offered him one of his cigars, and Sapirstone gave him one of his brand. After fifteen minutes they were talking as if they had known each other for years.

They had moved in the same circles in New York; both came from Poland. Sapirstone took out a wallet of alligator leather and showed Israel Danziger photographs of his wife, two daughters, two sons-in-law—one a doctor, one a lawyer—and several grandchildren. One granddaughter looked like a copy of Sapirstone. The woman was fat, like a Sabbath stewpot. Compared to her, his Hilda was a beauty. Danziger wondered how a man could live with such an ugly woman. On the other hand, he reflected, with one of her kind, you wouldn't be as lonesome as he was with Hilda. A woman like that would always have a swarm of chattering biddies around her.

Israel Danziger had never been pious, but since his heart attack and his retirement to Miami Beach he had begun to think in religious terms. Now he beheld the finger of God in his coming together with Morris Sapirstone.

"Do you play chess?" he asked.

"Chess, no. But I do play pinochle."

"Is there anybody to play with?"

"I find them."

"You're a smart man. I can't find anybody. I sit around all day long and don't see a soul."

"Why did you settle so far uptown?"

In the course of their talk Morris Sapirstone mentioned that there was a hotel for sale. It was almost a new hotel, all the way uptown. The owners had gone bankrupt, and the bank was ready to sell it for a song. All you needed was a quarter of a million in cash. Israel Danziger was far from ready for a business proposition, but he listened eagerly. Talk of money, credit, banks, and mortgages cheered him up. It was proof, somehow, that the world had not yet come to an end. Israel Danziger knew nothing at all about hotels, but he picked up bits of information from Morris Sapirstone's story. The owners of the hotel had failed because they sought a fancy clientele and made their rates too high. The rich people had stopped coming to Miami Beach. You had to attract the middle class. One good winter season and your investment would be covered. A new element was coming to Miami—the Latin Americans who chose Florida during the summer to "cool off." Israel Danziger groped in his shirt pocket for a pencil stub. While Morris went on talking, Israel wrote figures in the margin of his newspaper with great speed.

At the same time, he plied Sapirstone with questions. How many rooms in the hotel? How much can one room bring in? What about taxes? Mortgages? Personnel costs? For Israel, it was no more than a pastime, a reminder that once he, too, had been in business. He scratched his left temple with the point of the pencil.

"And what do you do if you have a bad season?"

"You have to see to it that it's good."

"How?"

"You have to advertise properly. Even in the Yiddish newspapers."

"Do they have a hall for conventions?"

AN HOUR HAD PASSED and Israel Danziger did not know where it had gone. He clenched his cigar between his lips and turned it busily around in his mouth. New strength welled up inside him. His heart, which in recent months had alternately fluttered and hesitated, now worked as if he were a healthy man. Morris Sapirstone took a small box from his coat pocket, picked out a pill, and swallowed it with a drink of water.

"You had an attack, eh?"

"Two."

"For whom do I need a hotel? For my wife's second husband?"

Morris Sapirstone did not answer.

"How can I get a look at this hotel?" Israel Danziger asked after a while.

"Come with me."

"Do you have a car here?"

"The red Cadillac across the street."

"Ah, a nice Cadillac you got."

The two men left the cafeteria. Israel Danziger noticed that Sapirstone was using a cane. Water in his legs, he thought. An invalid and he's hunting for hotels . . . Sapirstone settled behind the steering wheel and started the engine. He gave a whack to the car behind him, but he didn't even turn around. Soon he was racing along. One hand expertly grasped the steering wheel; with the other, he worked the cigarette lighter. With a cigar clamped in his teeth, he mumbled on.

"There's no charge for looking."

"No."

"If my wife hears about this, she'll give me plenty of trouble. Before you know it, she'll tell the doctor and then they'll both eat me up alive."

"They told you to rest, eh?"

"And if they told me? One must rest *here*, in the head. But my mind doesn't rest. I lie awake at night and think about all kinds of nothings. And when you're up you get hungry. My wife went to a locksmith to find out whether she can put a lock on the refrigerator . . . All these diets make you more sick than well. How did people live in the old days? In my time there were no diets. My grandfather, he should rest in peace, used to eat up a whole plateful of onions and chicken fat as an appetizer. Then he got busy on the soup with drops of fat floating on top. Next he had a fat piece of meat. And he finished up with a schmaltz cake. Where was cholesterol then? My grandfather lived to be eighty-seven, and he died because he fell on the ice one winter. Let me tell you: someday they'll find out that cholesterol is healthy. They'll be taking cholesterol tablets just as they take vitamin pills today."

"I wish you were right."

"A man is like a Hanukkah dreidel. It gets a turn, and then it spins on by itself until it drops."

"On a smooth table, it'll spin longer."

"There aren't any smooth tables."

The car stopped. "Well, that's the hotel."

Israel Danziger took one look and saw everything in a moment. If it was true that you only had to lay down a quarter of a million, the hotel was a fantastic bargain. Everything was new. It must have cost a fortune to build. Of course it was located a little too far uptown, but the center was moving uptown now. Once, the Gentiles ran away from the Jews. Now the Jews were running away from the Jews. Across the street there was already a kosher meat market. Israel Danziger rubbed his forehead. He would have to put in a hundred and twenty-five thousand dollars as his share. He could borrow that much from the bank, giving his stocks as security. He might even be able to scrape together the cash without a loan. But should he really get involved in such headaches? It would be suicide, sheer suicide. What would Hilda say? And Dr. Cohen? They'd all be at me—Hilda, the boys, the girls, their husbands. That in itself could lead to a second attack . . .

Israel Danziger closed his eyes and for a while remained enveloped in his own darkness. Like a fortune-teller, he tried to project himself into the future and foresee what fate had in store for him. His mind became blank, dark, overcome with the numbness of sleep. He even heard himself snore. All his affairs, his entire life, hung in the balance this second. He was waiting for a command from within, a voice from his own depths . . . Better to die than to go on living like this, he mumbled finally.

"What's the matter, Mr. Danziger, did you fall asleep?" he heard Sapirstone ask.

"Eh? No."

"So come in. Let's take a look at what's going on in here."

And the two little men climbed the steps to the fourteen-story hotel.

The tin door of the outhouse rattled shut and the German woman emerged into the sun again. Her towel had a wet stain. Mitchell put down his letter and crawled to the door of his hut. As soon as he stuck out his head, he could feel the heat. The sky was the filtered blue of a souvenir postcard, the ocean one shade darker. The white sand was like a tanning reflector. He squinted at the silhouette hobbling toward him.

"How are you feeling?"

The German woman didn't answer until she reached a stripe of shade between the huts. She lifted her foot and scowled at it. "When I go, it is just brown water."

"It'll go away. Just keep fasting."

"I am fasting three days now."

"You have to starve the amoebas out."

"*Ja*, but I think the amoebas are maybe starving me out." Except for the towel she was still naked, but naked like a sick person. Mitchell didn't feel anything. She waved and started walking away.

When she was gone, he crawled back into his hut and lay on the mat again. He picked up the pen and wrote, *Mohandas K. Gandhi used to sleep with his grandnieces, one on either side, to test his vow of chastity—i.e., saints are always fanatics.*

He laid his head on the bathing suit and closed his eyes. In a moment, the ringing started again.

IT WAS INTERRUPTED SOME TIME LATER by the floor shaking. The bamboo bounced under Mitchell's head and he sat up. In the doorway his traveling companion's face hung like a harvest moon. Larry was wearing a Burmese lungi and an Indian silk scarf. His chest, hairier than you expected on a little guy, was bare, and sunburned as pink as his face. His scarf had metallic gold and silver threads and was thrown dramatically over one shoulder. He was smoking a bidi, half bent over, looking at Mitchell.

"Diarrhea update," he said.

"I'm fine."

"You're fine?"

"I'm okay."

Larry seemed disappointed. The new pink skin on his forehead wrinkled. He held up a small glass bottle. "I brought you some pills. For the shits."

"Pills plug you up," Mitchell said. "Then the amoebas stay in you."

"Gwendolyn gave them to me. You should try them. Fasting would have worked by now. It's been what? Almost a week?"

"Fasting doesn't include being force-fed eggs."

"One egg," said Larry, waving this away.

"I was all right before I ate that egg. Now my stomach hurts."

"I though you said you were fine."

"I am fine," said Mitchell, and his stomach erupted. He felt a series of pops in his lower abdomen, followed his feet on the platform to either side of the hole. Then he closed the door and everything became dark. He undid his lungi and pulled it up, hanging the fabric around his neck. Using Asian toilets had made him limber: he could squat for ten minutes without strain. As for the smell, he hardly noticed it anymore. He held the door closed so that no one would barge in on him.

The sheer volume of liquid that rushed out of him still surprised him, but it always came as a relief. He imagined the amoebas being swept away in the flood, swirling down the drain of himself and out of his body. The dysentery had made him intimate with his insides; he had a clear sense of his stomach, of his colon; he felt the smooth muscular piping that constituted him. The combustion began high in his intestines. Then it worked its way along, like an egg swallowed by a snake, expanding, stretching the tissue, until, with a series of shudders, it dropped, and he exploded into water.

HE'D BEEN SICK NOT FOR A WEEK but for thirteen days. He hadn't said anything to Larry at first. One morning in a guesthouse in Bangkok, Mitchell had awoken with a queasy stomach. Once up and out of his mosquito netting, though, he'd felt better. Then that night after dinner, there'd come a series of taps, like fingers drumming on the inside of his abdomen. The next morning the diarrhea started. That was no big deal. He'd had it before in India, but it had gone away after a few days. This didn't. Instead, it got worse, sending him to the bathroom a few times after every meal. Soon he started to feel fatigued. He got dizzy when he stood up. His stomach burned after eating. But he kept on traveling. He didn't think it was anything serious. From Bangkok, he and Larry took a bus to the coast, where they boarded on a ferry to the island. The boat puttered into the small cove, shutting off its engine in the shallow water. They had to wade to shore. Just that—jumping in—had confirmed things. The sloshing of the sea mimicked the sloshing in Mitchell's gut. As soon as they got settled, Mitchell had begun to fast. For a week now he'd consumed nothing but black tea, leaving the hut only for the outhouse. Coming out one day, he'd run into the German woman and had persuaded her to start fasting, too. Otherwise, he lay on his mat, thinking and writing letters home.

231

Greetings from paradise. Larry and I are currently staying on a tropical island in the Gulf of Siam (check the world atlas). We have our own hut right on the beach, for which we pay the princely sum of five dollars per night. The island hasn't been discovered yet so there's almost nobody here. He went on, describing the island (or as much as he could glimpse through the bamboo), but soon returned to more important preoccupations. *Eastern religion teaches that all matter is illusory. That includes everything, our house, every one of Dad's suits, even Mom's plant hangers—all* maya, *according to the Buddha. That category also includes, of course, the body. One of the reasons I decided to take this Grand Tour was that our frame of reference back in Detroit seemed a little cramped. And there are a few things I've come to believe in. And to test. One of which is that we can control our bodies with our minds. They have monks in Tibet who can mentally regulate their physiologies. They play a game called "melting snowballs." They put a snowball in one hand and then meditate, sending all their internal heat to that hand. The one who melts the snowball fastest wins.*

From time to time, he stopped writing to sit with his eyes closed, as though waiting for inspiration. And that was exactly how he'd been sitting two months earlier—eyes closed, spine straight, head lifted, nose somehow alert—when the ringing started. It had happened in a pale green Indian hotel room in Mahalibalipuram. Mitchell had been sitting on his bed, in the half-lotus position. His inflexible left, western knee stuck way up in the air. Larry was off exploring the streets. Mitchell was all alone. He hadn't even been waiting for anything to happen. He was just sitting there, trying to meditate, his mind wandering to all sorts of things. For instance, he was thinking about his old girlfriend, Christine Woodhouse, and her amazing red pubic hair that he'd never get to see again. He was thinking about food. He was hoping they had something in this town besides *idli sambar*. Every so often he'd become aware of how much his mind was wandering, and then he'd try to direct it back to his breathing. Then sometime in the middle of all this, when he least expected it, when he'd stopped even trying or waiting for anything to happen (which was exactly when all the mystics said it would happen), Mitchell's ears had begun to ring. Very softly. It wasn't an unfamiliar ringing. In fact, he recognized it. He

232

could remember standing in the front yard one day as a little kid and suddenly hearing this ringing in his ears, and asking his older brothers, "Do you hear that ringing?" They said they didn't but knew what he was talking about. In the pale green hotel room, after almost twenty years, Mitchell heard it again. He thought maybe this ringing was what they meant by the Cosmic Om. Or the music of the spheres. He kept trying to hear it after that. Wherever he went, he listened for the ringing, and after a while he got pretty good at hearing it. He heard it in the middle of Sudder Street in Calcutta, with cabs honking and street urchins shouting for baksheesh. He heard it on the train up to Chiang Mai. It was the sound of the universal energy, of all the atoms linking up to create the colors before his eyes. It had been right there the whole time. All he had to do was wake up and listen to it.

233

He wrote home, at first tentatively, then with growing confidence, about what was happening to him. *The energy flow of the universe is capable of being perceived. We are, each of us, finely tuned radios. We just have to blow the dust off our tubes.* He sent his parents a few letters each week. He sent letters to his brothers, too. And to his friends. Whatever he was thinking, he wrote down. He didn't consider people's reactions. He was seized by a need to analyze his intuitions, to describe what he saw and felt. *Dear Mom and Dad, I saw a woman being cremated this afternoon. You can tell if it's a woman by the color of the shroud. Hers was red. It burned off first. Then her skin did. While I was watching, her intestines filled up with hot gas, like a great big balloon. They got bigger and bigger until they finally popped. Then all this fluid came out. I tried to find something similar on a postcard for you but no such luck.*

Or else: *Dear Petie, Does it ever occur to you that this world of earwax remover and embarrassing jock itch might not be the whole megillah? Sometimes it looks that way to me. Blake believed in angelic recitation. And who knows? His poems back him up. Except for that one about the lamb, which I've always hated. Sometimes at night, though, when the moon gets that very pale thing going, I swear I feel a flutter against the three-day growth on my cheeks.*

Mitchell had called home only once, from Calcutta. The connection had been bad. It was the first time Mitchell and his parents had experienced the transatlantic delay. His father answered. Mitchell said hello, hearing nothing until his last syllable, the *o*, echoed in his ears. After that, the static changed registers, and his father's voice came through. Traveling over half the globe, it lost some of its characteristic force. "Now listen, your mother and I want you to get on a plane and get yourself back home."

"I just got to India."

"You've been gone six months. That's long enough. We don't care what it costs. Use that credit card we gave you and buy yourself a ticket back home."

"I'll be home in two months or so."

"What the hell are you doing over there?" his father shouted, as best as he could, against the satellite. "What is this about dead bodies in the Ganges? You're liable to come down with some disease."

"No, I won't. I feel fine."

"Well, you mother doesn't feel fine. She's worried half to death."

"Dad, this the best part of the trip so far. Europe was great and everything, but it's still the West."

"And what's wrong with the West?"

"Nothing. Only it's more exciting to get away from your own culture."

"Speak to your mother," his father said.

And then his mother's voice, almost a whimper, had come over the line. "Mitchell, are you okay?"

"I'm fine."

"We're worried about you."

"Don't worry. I'm *fine*."

"You don't sound right in your letters. What's going on with you?"

Mitchell wondered if he could tell her. But there was no way to say it. You couldn't say, I've found the truth. People didn't like that.

"You sound like one of those Hare Krishnas."

"I haven't joined up yet, Mom. So far, all I've done is shave my head."

"You shaved your head, Mitchell!"

"No," he told her, though in fact it was true: he had shaved his head.

Then his father was back on the line. His voice was strictly business now, a gutter voice Mitchell hadn't heard before. "Listen, stop cocking around over there in India

The strange thing was that here, in the hut, verifiably sick, Mitchell had never felt so good, so tranquil, or so brilliant in his life. He felt secure and watched over in a way he couldn't explain. He felt *happy*. Not so the German woman. She looked worse and worse. She hardly spoke when they passed now. Her skin looked even paler, splotchier. After a while Mitchell stopped encouraging her to keep fasting. He lay on his back, with the bathing suit over his eyes now, and paid no attention to her trips to the outhouse. He listened instead to the sounds of the island, people swimming and shouting on the beach, somebody learning to play a wooden flute a few huts down. Waves lapped, and occasionally a dead palm leaf or coconut fell to the ground. At night, the wild dogs began howling in the jungle. When he went to the outhouse, Mitchell could hear them moving around outside, coming up and sniffing him, the flow of his waste, through the holes in the walls. Most people banged flashlights against the tin door to scare the dogs away. Mitchell didn't even bring a flashlight along. He stood listening to the dogs gather in the vegetation. With sharp muzzles they pushed stalks aside until their red eyes appeared in the moonlight. Mitchell faced them down, serenely. He spread out his arms, offering himself, and when they didn't attack, turned and walked back to his hut.

One night as he was coming back, he heard an Australian voice say, "Here comes the patient now." He looked up to see Larry and an older woman sitting on the porch of the hut. Larry was rolling a joint on his *Let's Go: Asia*. The woman

238

was smoking a cigarette and looking straight at Mitchell. "Hello, Mitchell, I'm Gwendolyn," she said. "I hear you've been sick."

"Somewhat."

"Larry says you haven't been taking the pills I sent over."

Mitchell didn't answer right away. He hadn't talked to another human being all day. Or for a couple of days. He had to get reacclimated. Solitude had sensitized him to the roughness of other people, too. Gwendolyn's loud whisky baritone, for instance, seemed to rake right across his chest. She was wearing some kind of batik headdress that looked like a bandage. Lots of tribal jewelry, too, bones and shells, hanging around her neck and from her wrists. In the middle of all this was her pinched, oversunned face, with the red coil of the cigarette in the center blinking on and off. Larry was just a halo of blond hair in the moonlight.

"I had a terrible case of the trots myself," Gwendolyn continued. "Truly epic. In Irian Jaya. Those pills were a godsend."

Larry gave a finishing lick to the joint and lit it. He inhaled, looking up at Mitchell, then said in a smoke-tightened voice, "We're here to make you take your medicine."

"That's right. Fasting is all well and good, but after—what has it been?"

"Two weeks almost."

"After two weeks, it's time to stop." She looked stern,

really keen and intelligent looking. It was sort of warm. *She touched her arm-knobs together, to thank me. And right then my coin hit the cup, and her son, who maybe couldn't see, said, "Atcha." He said it in a very pleased sort of way, almost smiling, though it was hard to tell if he was smiling because of the way his face was melting off. But what happened right then was this: I saw that they were people, not beggars or terribly unfortunate bad-karma types or anything like that—but just a mother and her kid. I could sort of see them back before they got leprosy or whatever, back when they used to just go out for a walk. And then I had another kind of revelation. I had a hunch that that kid was a nut for mango lassis. And this seemed a very profound revelation to me at the time. It was as big a revelation as I think I ever need or deserve. When my coin hit the cup and the boy said, "Atcha," I just knew that he was thinking about a nice cold mango lassi.* Mitchell put down his pen, remembering. Then he went outside to watch the sunset. He sat down on the porch cross-legged. His left knee no longer stuck up. When he closed his eyes, the ringing began at once, louder, more intimate, more ravishing than ever.

SO MUCH SEEMED FUNNY when viewed from this distance. His worries about choosing a major. The way he used to not even leave the house when afflicted with glaring facial pimples. Even the searing despair of the time he'd called Christine Woodhouse's room and she hadn't come in all night was sort of funny now. You could waste your life. He had, pretty much, until the day he'd boarded that airplane with Larry, inoculated against typhus and cholera, and had escaped. Only now, with no one watching, could Mitchell find out who he was. It was as though riding in all those buses, over all those bumps, his old self had become dislodged bit by bit, so that it just rose up one day and vaporized into the Indian air. He didn't want to go back to the world of college and clove cigarettes. He was lying on his back, waiting for the moment when the body touched against enlightenment, or when nothing happened at all, which would be the same thing.

Meanwhile, next door, the German woman was on the move again. Mitchell heard her rustling around. She came down her steps, but instead of heading for the outhouse, she climbed the steps to Mitchell's hut. He removed the bathing suit from his eyes.

"I am going to the clinic. In the boat."

"I figured you might."

"I am going to get an injection. Stay one night. Then come back." She paused for a moment. "You want to come with me? Get an injection?"

"No, thanks."

"Why not?"

"Because I'm better. I'm feeling a lot better."

"Come to the clinic. To be safe. We go together."

"I'm fine." He stood up, smiling, to indicate this. Out in the bay, the boat blew its horn.

Mitchell came out onto the porch to send her off. "I'll keep the home fires burning," he said. The German woman waded out to the boat and climbed aboard. She stood on accomplished tans and fetching accents. They kept coming up to encircle his wrists with their thumbs and forefingers. "I'd die for cheekbones like yours," one girl said. Then she made him eat some fried bananas.

Night fell. Somebody announced a party in hut number six. Before Mitchell knew what was happening, he was being escorted by two Dutch girls down the beach. They waitressed in Amsterdam five months of the year and spent the rest traveling. Apparently, Mitchell looked exactly like a van Hanthorst Christ in the Rijksmuseum. The Dutch girls found the resemblance both awe inspiring and hilarious. Mostly hilarious. Mitchell started wondering if he'd made a mistake by staying in the hut. Some kind of tribal life had started up here on the island. No wonder Larry'd been having such a good time. Everybody was so friendly. It wasn't even sexual so much as just warm and intimate. One of the Dutch girls had a nasty rash on her back she turned around to show him.

The moon was already rising over the bay, casting a long swath of light in to shore. It lit up the trunks of palm trees and gave the sand a lunar phosphorescence. Everything was blue except for the orange, glowing huts. Mitchell felt the air rinsing his face and flowing through his legs as he walked. There was a lightness inside him, a helium balloon around his heart. There was nothing a person needed beyond this beach.

He called out, "Hey, Larry." Larry was just up ahead. "What?"

"We've gone everywhere, man."

"Not everywhere. Next stop Bali."

"Then home. After Bali, home. Before my parents have a nervous breakdown."

He stopped suddenly, holding the Dutch girls back. He thought he heard the ringing—louder than ever—but then realized that it was just the music coming from hut number six. Right out front, people were sitting in a circle in the sand. They made room for Mitchell and the new arrivals.

"What do you say, doctor? Can we give him a beer?"

"Very funny," the medical student said. "I suggest one. No more."

In due course, the beer was passed along the fire brigade and into Mitchell's hands. Then the person to Mitchell's right put her hand on his knee. It was Gwendolyn. He hadn't recognized her in the darkness. She took a long drag on her cigarette. She turned her face away, to exhale primarily, but also with the suggestion of hurt feelings, and said, "You haven't thanked me."

"For what?"

"For the pills."

"Oh, right. That was really thoughtful of you and everything."

She smiled for about four seconds and then started coughing. It was a smoker's cough, with gravel shifting around inside. She tried to suppress it by leaning forward and covering her mouth, but it didn't help. The coughs just echoed inside her chest cavity. Finally they stopped, and she wiped her eyes. "Oh, I'm dying." She looked around the circle of people. Everyone was talking and laughing. "Nobody cares."

All this time Mitchell had been examining Gwendolyn closely. It seemed clear to him that if she didn't have lung cancer already, she was going to get it soon. "Do you want to know how I knew you were separated?" he said.

"Well, I think I might."

"It's because of this glow you have. Women who get divorced or separated always have this glow. I've noticed it before. It's like they get younger or something."

"Really?"

"Yes, indeed," said Mitchell.

Gwendolyn smiled. "I am feeling rather restored."

Mitchell held out his beer and they clinked bottles.

"Cheers," she said.

"Cheers." He took a sip of beer. It was the best beer he'd ever tasted. Suddenly he felt ecstatically happy. There wasn't a campfire in the center, warming everyone, but it felt like that. Mitchell squinted at all the different faces and then just looked out at the bay. He thought about his trip. He tried to remember all the places he and Larry had gone, all the smelly pensions, the baroque cities, the hill stations. If he didn't think about any single place, he could sort of feel them all, kaleidoscopically shifting around inside his head. He felt complete and satisfied. At some point the ringing had started up again, and he was concentrating on that, too, so that at first he didn't notice the twinge in his intestines. Then, from far off, piercing his consciousness, came another twinge, still so delicate that he might have imagined it. In a moment it came again, more insistently. He felt a valve open inside him, and a trickle of hot liquid, like acid, begin burning its way toward the outside. He wasn't alarmed. He felt too good. He just stood up again and said, "I'm going down to the water a minute."

"I'll go with you," said Larry.

The moon was higher now. As they approached, the bay was lit up like a mirror. Away from the music, Mitchell could hear the wild dogs barking in the jungle. He led Larry straight down to the water's edge. Then, without pausing, he let his lungi drop and stepped out of it. He waded out.

"Skinny-dip?"

Mitchell didn't answer.

"What's the water temp?"

"Cold," said Mitchell, though this wasn't true: the water was warm. It was only that he wanted to be alone in it for some reason. He waded out until the water was waist deep. Cupping both hands, he sprinkled water over his face. Then he dropped into the water and began to float on his back.

His ears plugged up. He heard water rushing, then the silence of the sea, then the ringing again. It was clearer than ever. It wasn't a ringing so much as a beacon penetrating his body.

He lifted his head and said, "Larry."

"What?"

"Thanks for taking care of me."

"No problem."

Now that he was in the water, he felt better again. He sensed the pull of the tide out in the bay, retreating with the night wind and the rising moon. A small hot stream came out of him, and he paddled away from it and continued to float. He stared up at the sky. He didn't have his pen or aerograms with him, so he began to dictate silently: *Dear Mom and Dad, The earth itself is all the evidence we need. Its rhythms, its perpetual regeneration, the rising and falling of the moon, the tide flowing in to land and out again to sea, all this is a lesson for that very slow learner, the human race. The earth keeps repeating the drill, over and over, until we get it right.*

252

"Nobody would believe this place," Larry said on the beach. "It's a total fucking paradise."

The ringing grew louder. A minute passed, or a few minutes. Finally he heard Larry say, "Hey, Mitch, I'm going back to the party now. You okay?" He sounded far away.

Mitchell stretched out his arms, which allowed him to float a little higher on the water. He couldn't tell if Larry had gone or not. He was looking at the moon. He'd begun to notice something about the moon that he'd never noticed before. He could make out the wavelengths of the moonlight. He'd managed to slow his mind down enough to perceive that. The moonlight would speed up a second, growing brighter, then it would slow down, becoming dim. It *pulsed.* The moonlight was a kind of ringing itself. He lay undulating in the warm water, observing the correspondence of moonlight and ringing, how they increased together, diminished together. After a while, he began to be aware that he, too, was like that. His blood pulsed with the moonlight, with the ringing. Something was coming out of him, far away. He felt his insides emptying out. The sensation of water leaving him was no longer painful or explosive; it had become a steady flow of his essence into nature. In the next second, Mitchell felt as though he were dropping through the water, and then he had no sense of himself at all. He wasn't the one looking at the moon or hearing the ringing. And yet he was aware of them. For a moment, he thought he should send word to his parents, to tell them not to worry. He'd found the paradise beyond the island. He was trying to gather himself to dictate this last message, but soon he realized that there was nothing left of him to do it—nothing at all—no person left to hold a pen or to send word to the people he loved, who would never understand.